# Front cover:

**Top picture: Dottie Walsh & Ben Archer 1962**

**Bottom Picture:  Ben and Pendron Archer circa 1947**

## Table of Contents

# Introduction

# Afterword

# From Here To Puberty

## Introduction

It all began in September 1953 when I was eight years old. My parents decided to give me a Catholic education so they sent me to Saint Barnabas in a suburb of Chicago. The teachers were nuns with black habits and white bibs. Quite happily and unbeknownst to me at this age, the kids around me, my peers, the children I would get to know and grow up with, were for the most part, Irish.

I was surrounded with kids named Boyle, Brogan, Casey, Connelly, Flanagan, Gallagher, Murdock, and of course, the many "O's," O'Donnell, O'Malley, O'Connor, O'Hara. As a boy of eight, I looked around and saw kids roughly my age and height, mostly white but did not think Irishness was important. What was important to me was how bright they were, how fast they could run, how honest they were and who was the funniest. I did not realize it then but these kids were to be my formational bedrock, the start of life, what life was like, the basic normal. I made friends with many of them and still know them and speak regularly to them after half a century. They were my "hood."

My suburb was wealthy. The homes were large, some of them outright mansions but mine wasn't. My mother called it "The Shoe," after the Mother Goose rhyme:

*"There was an old woman who lived in a shoe. She had so many children, she didn't know what to do. She gave them some broth without any bread. And whipped them all soundly and put them to bed."*

My mom thought she was like this old lady because she had five kids and some of the other aspects of the rhyme reminded her of our situation.

The lawns were spacious and all needed regular mowing in the hot, humid Midwestern summers. I cut many lawns as I grew up. I hated it but I became competent at it and made good money during the summers between my high school years. Before I was old enough to mow lawns I weeded gardens and raked leaves. I made the princely sum of 75 cents an hour. The wealth aspect of our suburb was something that never left me. It affected us in so many ways. How people spoke, what they wore, how they created, entered and left cliques, all were informed by wealth. Most of the men were successful businessmen, CEO's or presidents of their own companies. Around the corner from my house lived a well-known Cub baseball player. One of the kids in my class had an Air Force general for a father. One day the general arranged for us to be driven out to O'Hare Field. When we arrived at O'Hare the general was dressed in a flight suit. We stood around his T-33 "T-bird" jet and watched as he did a walk-around inspection. With the help of an airman he climbed into the front seat, waved goodbye to us and off he taxied to the loud whine of the jet engine. Several minutes later we heard the distant roar of his jet spool up to full power and he took off, a huge cloud of dirty exhaust coming from the back end of his jet. We learned later he landed at Washington DC about 55 minutes later.

I never knew what most of my peers' fathers did for a living. Mr. Connor was a tall, handsome man who, every time there was an occasion for a grand, powerful tenor at Catholic Church ceremonies, he would sing from a podium in the front of the church. He was a magnificent singer and lived in a big house but I never learned his occupation. Music was one of the best parts of my six years at St. Barnabas. Roman Catholicism is full of mysticism, incense, ceremony and glorious music, all of which I was fully instructed in as I grew up. By the time I was twelve, I was making $10.00 per wedding to sing in the back of the church with Father O'Donnelly, most frequently, *Ave Maria* for baritone and tenor. He was a tall, patient priest who taught me Gregorian Chant and musical notation. Music was glorious. I shall wax on how important it was in my life in later chapters.

During my six years at St. Barnabas, I grew up with all the other kids and encountered the sports of the day, the phobias, the folklore, "da babes." Girls became an obsession for most of us, but there were flashes of intellectual development too. My family was a Roman Catholic family, not eating meat on Friday, going-to-church-on-Sunday family. I was an early and voracious reader. Reading ultimately, (And the thinking it stimulated) turned me off Catholicism. By age ten I became a firm atheist. But how a "firm atheist" worked his way around all the Catholics, both my age and adults, I will tell you.

I wanted to be a fighter pilot and fly the gleaming F-86 Sabre Jet,
A beautiful F-86 Sabre Jet on display in Hawaii:

but I also wanted to be a nuclear physicist like my hero Dr. Enrico Fermi. He split the atom underneath Stagg Field House at the University of Chicago in 1942 and created the first sustained nuclear reaction…and lived through it! I also wanted to be an opera singer like my hero Ezio Pinza too. I idolized Mickey Mantle of the Yankees and Notre Dame Football players like Al Ecuyer and Nick Pietrosante, All-Americans of 1958, which typified my age group then. But I simultaneously wanted to sing at the Metropolitan Opera as a bass and sing operatic duets with Mario Lanza and Roberta Peters.

8

This saga will be an account of the many funny incidents, the discoveries of childhood growing problems, discovering the mysteries of sex, the life long pleasure/ worry for Catholics. It will also be about sports, music, making and losing friends and the immense social pressures brought upon young men of my generation.

Do you remember the very popular 1986 motion picture *Stand By Me* directed by Rob Reiner, starring River Phoenix and Will Wheaton? It was about four young boys growing up in a rural town in Oregon in the Fifties who learn a boy was killed by a train and decide to trek out overnight to find the body. Reiner nailed the boys' development. They were alternately childish, winsome, scared, and cocky. Each had his own distinct personality, which we, as viewers. could easily identify with. My kids loved *Stand By Me* too. We all did. I grew up in the exact same time period, the Fifties and I had friends and boyhood adventures almost exactly parallel to the kids in *Stand By Me*. My friends and I, at about age 12, even went down to the railroad area where we heard a woman was killed by a train to look for body parts. I remember one of my friends yelling, "I got dibs on an eye!" I also remember getting slapped across the face by one of the nuns for objecting to the lecture a big, dumb cop gave us for doing so. We nicknamed the cop "Brom Bones" and we got our symbolic revenge on him. That story will come later in this book.

But there was much more to growing up in the Fifties than merely doing kid-like things. The Fifties started out with a bang...literally. The Korean War and the ongoing Cold War with Russia, the notion of building an underground dwelling to escape a huge nuclear blast, the Nike sites around Chicago, the serious and ongoing examination of Catholic theology. All of these things and events I observed and dealt with in my mind and compared them to what existed in my friends' minds. There was the famous discussion I initiated with the Right Reverend, Monsignor Allen Hilbert at the rectory one day when I was ten about the existence of God. My first mad crush on a girl, my first sexual feelings and the resistance the Catholic church put up and our school boy reactions to it; these form major parts of my book.

Most of my siblings, with the exception of Pendron, who was a master athlete and maker of things with his hands, had musical leanings. Bruno played the French horn well enough to be first chair at Lakeside High School and later at his university. Aubere sang at Lakeside in the Opera group and had major parts in the light operas produced there. Woban had a wonderful soprano voice and could memorize lyrics very quickly. Plus she earned the lead in *Amahl and the Night Visitors* I will write about later. There were beautiful times I remember as a boy of five or six. I would be lying on my back underneath our baby grand piano, bare feet up gently pressing against the bottom of the piano while Woban played Beethoven's *Fur Elise,* Bruno accompanying her on his French horn which he named "Freddy." The vibrations from these sessions worked their way down my feet into my whole body, into my very being. I simply loved music.


It was about age six or seven that I became a young pyromaniac, Twice I set fires at home the fire department had to come to the rescue. I had not meant to do it. I was playing with matches. We used to light them and throw them at each other. Was I a total idiot? Or is this merely one of the things boys do? The back porch was where we sometimes slept during the summer months. It was a screened in, large, rectangular room on the north side of our home. My mother had a basket in which she kept her crocheting materials. I was lighting matches with a neighbor boy and my last throw missed him and landed in the crocheting. But I did not see it because we were running around like mad, each trying to get the other guy. I was dodging and throwing alternately.

About 20 minutes after we were playing in the back porch I heard the fire trucks coming. I knew instantly what had happened and hid behind the couch in our front room. I remember being able to see the Fire Marshall's big black boots from underneath the couch as he stood in front of the couch talking to my mother. "Where is that little fire-starter boy of yours?" The tone of his loud, commanding voice completely terrified me. I thought he would take me away in his fire truck and maybe let the fire dog bite me.

The second time I lit a fire was in my kitchen during dinner. I lit a match and thought someone was coming so I threw it into a large waste basket which was beneath a table. Then I went back to the dinner table and sat there innocently eating my dinner. In about ten minutes the smell of smoke became obvious and my brothers raced into the kitchen to find the table and wall behind it in a major conflagration. They threw water at it and called the fire department. That time it was only one wall and a table but they were really burned. The odd part about the second fire was that I don't remember what happened next. I think it was partly that my parents suspected my grandmother who was very, old might have started it.

I would be remiss if I did not provide you with a glossary of all the crazy names I gave my family and how most of them stuck. Years later my wife was taken back by the kind of names that we all used. She asked me, "Did you grow up in a suburb of Chicago or a menagerie?" Here is the list:

| Relationship | Nickname |
| --- | --- |
| Grandmother | Nudie Nundie |
| Aunt | Wow Mow |
| Father | Chief |
| Mother | Zombie |
| Oldest Brother | Bruno |
| Brother 2ed oldest | Aubere |
| Sister | Woban |
| 3rd Brother | Pendron |

I will introduce you to each of these family members as the occasion warrants. You might ask, what did people call me? I did not care as long as it was polite. You see, I had and still have this tendency to make up nicknames for everyone I deal with. If I have given you a nickname, it means I think you are important enough to matter.

I invite you Dear Reader, to sit back and enjoy the following memories from that era. I will take you from 1953 when I was eight to 1963 when I graduated from high school. The names and places have been altered to protect the innocent and guilty (By Catholic standards we were all guilty and would be going to hell at least according to the nuns!) I imagine, whether or not you went to a Catholic school, you will be able to find parallels to your youth. My four years in high school were at a government school, a public school financed by taxes. This four-year event I shall mine for funny incidents and some serious ideas.

# Chapter One The Catholic Awakening

I still vividly remember my first impressions of St. Barnabas Catholic School over 50 years later. The look, the green boards which used yellow chalk instead of blackboards that my former government/public school had. I even remember the smells of the new classroom. I was placed in third grade with Miss Schmidt, a "lay" teacher instead of a nun. I would not get an actual nun as a teacher until fourth grade. I walked to school and found it to be exactly one mile and two tenth each way. I would walk most of the time, get a ride with my father sometimes, and ride my bike in good weather, Best of all, a very pretty girl, Mary O'Sullivan, a girl I would fall head over heals with, lived in a direct line of my path to my new school. I found myself walking her there and back many times over the next six years. Soon the shenanigans began. All the classrooms were appointed with little chairs and desks which grew slightly larger as we got older. The chair and desk were separate. We boys found that if we placed a book on our knees and then placed the book directly in the center of the desk we could lift the desk off the floor by an inch or so. This was to generate into a sexual joke. The Catholic teachers trained us to all stand when any adult entered our classroom, especially if the adult was a priest or nun.

But we stood for all adults as an expression of respect. As we grew older we would lift our desks on our knees when a good looking woman came in, the better looking she was the higher the desks went. I don't remember ever being caught doing this but we found it hilarious. Did I personally go along with this? Well, yes, in fact I led it.

In Third grade I met Carlos "Malbun" Danks, a red-haired, fun-loving, very athletic boy my age. He lived next to the local golf course and had a dog that scared me to death and a sister with Cerebral Palsy who also scared me to death, at least at first. "Malbun" as I called him, would be one of my life long friends. His mother used to speak to me very seriously every time I left his house to peddle my bike home, "Now watch both ways when you get to the main road." she would say, "Tell me you will do this Ben!" And I did look both ways because I did not relish the idea of becoming guacamole on the front end of a large truck.

Over the next 60 years Malbun never ceased being my friend, even though he had a silly dislike of another friend I made at St. Barnabas. The other friend I began calling "Boy," (And he called me the same for the next 50 years.) I would ask Malbun what was the source of his dislike for Boy. He would say something like "Dislike? I hate the guy. I want to punch him out so badly." "But why?" I would persist, "What did he do to you?" I never could get an answer out of him on that issue. Gradually as we went through grammar school and high school Malbun's "hatred" mellowed to a low level disinterest.

Malbun and I literally grew up together. We confronted the intricacies of the Roman Catholic Church, we sang in the parish choir, we talked endlessly about girls and how to deal with them. We went on double dates in our high school years. We engaged in constant games of football, baseball, softball in the park, swimming at the beach and golf in high school. Even though he moved almost a thousand miles away at the end of high school, we never were estranged. He was a loyal friend for over 60 years until his death. He was also my great friend to whom nothing was hidden. All that time he had this magical capacity to make me laugh, not with jokes but quick verbal jabs at whatever we were discussing. Then he would laugh and bump elbows with me.

One of the issues Malban and I discussed during the next six years we were at St. Barnabas was one of many Catholic teachings from the nuns. The issue of the *Horror of Hell* thrust upon us if we were to steal so much as a pack of bubble gum from the local five and dime and get hit by a bus and killed as we ran out. The nuns insisted we would spend all eternity in the Lake of Fire, our skin roasting and being renewed by the Devil so it could roast again...forever! We thought this a bit much for stealing a ten cent pack of gum.

There were two other related issues that I observed about my peers' reaction to Catholicism. The first was that while many of them (in grammar school through high school) objected to the Virgin Birth, or Walking on Water or Turning Water into Wine, the well known little miracles performed by Christ, I never ran into a single Catholic who questioned the existence of God in the first place. The lack of questioning His existence held during my six years at St. Barnabas and four in high school. I reasoned that if an all-powerful god existed in the first place he would easily be able to do all the miracles. It was His existence itself that I pondered deeply.

Which brings us to another part of my being. Even as a young boy, I was acutely aware of certain philosophical issues. I think this was partly innate and partly due to background.

My background at home turned me toward ideas, books, concepts, humor, laughter...what Socrates called, "The Examined Life." As a very young boy, perhaps five or six, I would creep down the steps after I had been ordered to bed, to listen to my father and oldest brother Bruno reading Homer's *Odyssey*. They did this in the front room where we had a fire place flanked on both sides by book shelves that contained the entire Harvard Classics. My father had a warm baritone voice and I can remember it distinctly as he rolled his R's and had a lot of fun with long Greek names found in Homer. My oldest brother, would laugh and imitate him. From this I concluded that the "The Examined Life" not only was proper and necessary but it was also fun! 59 years later, Mary O'Sullivan, the girl I had frequently walked to school, suggested this when I bumped into her in Los Angeles in 2009. She told me, "You were a really weird kid, always asking questions that adults ask, always dealing with issues I did not understand." by which she meant, *philosophical* issues.

My very early philosophical leaning might have been innate too. I remember as early as seven lying on my bed thinking, "Gee, I'm alive and am aware of being alive. What a great notion! I'm Ben and separate from my brothers and yet can function with and without them. Already at that tender age I had observed my schoolmates and asked myself, "Why do they follow each other around so easily like trained dogs?" Later I heard one of my teachers use the word "conformity" in a derisive manner and I wanted to know what that meant. I asked my mother. She told me conformity meant 'following others without thinking first.' I looked the word up in the dictionary and got something like "compliance or acquiescence; obedience" but I did not understand those big words at age seven or eight. I *did* understand the word "blind." I did not want to live my life blindly.

The next happy find at my new Catholic school was that it was in a nice, safe suburban setting but a block away was a little commercial area with a five and dime store, coffee house and a large park next to it. I grew up at that park. I would spend hundreds and hundreds of hours over the next ten years playing and socializing there. We played softball, football and in the winter, when the park was flooded, many more hours ice skating.

My Old Man was from southern Ohio, an area my mom hinted was a bit on the rube side. Why was this? Well, my father's idea of a honeymoon was to take my mom on a car trip from Chicago to Washington DC and back where he was best remembered for successfully imitating the sounds of farm animals and stopping for a round of golf at every opportunity. And the food he prepared at home was equally memorable..

His most famous creation was "Cornmeal Mush." He would get a very large pot (Remember he was often making this for five kids and two or more adults.) and mix yellow cornmeal with water bringing it up under a medium heat until it was a thick, mushy....well...mush. The mush at this stage could be eaten as breakfast in a bowl with syrup but he was not finished yet. While the mush was cooling in the pot he prepared several, large pans with a coating of bacon grease. The bacon grease was kept in a large, old Folger's Coffee can on the stove. When the mush had reached his desired consistency, he would ladle it out on the pans and fry the mush into patties perhaps 3" X 2" and place them on plates. This was fresh, fried Corn-meal Mush and was often eaten at this stage with butter and syrup. But he was *still* not done. On another pan with bacon grease he fried sunny-side-up eggs and would place one on each corn meal mush patty. This was his Crowning Glory. We kids liked it a lot! If accompanied with three, well done strips of bacon, all the better.

My mom hated all this. While she was supposed to have a good deal because she did not have to cook breakfast, Chief used every pot and pan in the joint and managed to spray grease all over the stove and walls. She had to clean it up!

The next dish was much more simple. My Old Man introduced us to his favorite snack: peanut butter and onions on crackers. Sometimes for the more adventurous, it would be peanut butter, onions and *thin slices of Dill Pickle* on crackers. His Mush was a common meal of many people in the US in the 1950's and earlier. But peanut butter, onions, pickles on crackers seemed to be an original with Chief. And we loved this snack too. I still make it to this day, over a half century since he introduced it to me. Bruno disputes this version of my memory. He thinks *he* popularized peanut butter, crackers and onions. Aubere remembers Pendron cutting onion slices so thin that one could see through them!

For most Midwesterners corn-on-the-cob was a summer staple. We loved it. On summer afternoons Chief would take one or more of us in his company car about four miles directly west of our pad to abundant corn fields which, to me, as a seven year old, seemed to stretch out forever. Chief had a friend who worked at the corn stand and would get as many ears as Chief ordered ready and we would carry them to the car. I think Chief paid about 69 cents per dozen for them, maybe even less. We would have all these ears shucked and into giant kettles of boiling water within minutes of getting home.

Then the meal would consist mainly of buttered and salted corn-on-the-cob, ice tea, usually, and a salad of lettuce, tomato and other seasonal stuff. I remember eating eleven ears of giant, Midwestern corn-on-the-cob. in one sitting. One of the few regrets I have about living for most of my adult life in the extreme western part of the US is those monstrous, delicious, over-a-foot-long ears of Illinois corn. Corn is grown in the west but it's just not the same.

By third grade I had already been totally seduced by a music form that made me a bit of a soloist as a child. My brother made a crystal radio set. It consisted of a crystal, a kind of small irregular black rock about 2 centimeters square, a short needle and attached to it were two wires which came back into an earphone which my father had brought home from work. To receive radio stations one would gently move the needle about the crystal and, as if by magic, certain parts of it would bring in various stations. Late-night sessions yielded really good quality reception. We lived about 18 miles or so from downtown Chicago and we could receive AM radio stations on my brother's crystal set. I distinctly remember Christmas time, about 1953, when I heard Handel's *Messiah* for the first time. The soprano was Roberta Peters. I was stunned by the power and beauty of her voice. I also loved the tenor and bass parts too. Thus began a life-long super enjoyment of opera, symphonic music and classical/romantic music in general. And this was at the start of the Rock and Roll Era!

While most of my peers for the next six years were humming and jiving to pop music, I made a beeline for the orchestra and the operatic voice. Fortunately we had one of the greatest bands in the world to admire nearby...the Chicago Symphony Orchestra. I did not hide my love of classical music but my Irish pals simply had no ear for it. I was alone in this until I made a friend I called "Wonder" in high school who also loved symphonic music. Wonder eventually became a full time music director and conductor of his own symphony orchestra in northern Minnesota. I still love opera and symphonies 50 years later.

# Chapter Two The Plot Thickens

The summer before Fourth Grade I enjoyed the warmth of a Midwest summer, dug weeds out of neighbor's gardens, learned that I tend toward Teutonic thoroughness, which is not always a good thing, and drank gallons of ice tea that my mother served at dinner in large carafes. In fact I drank so much that I used to get up at night and pee in corners by mistake instead of the toilet. My brother Aubere would get after me to clean up the mess. One time he accused me of peeing on his legs but I don't know if I really did it.

One summer day all of my family went on a day trip in the car, except Nudie Nundie, my grandmother. When we arrived home we found all the doors locked tight, something that we rarely if ever did. One of my brothers had to climb in a dormer window and then open the door for us. After we were all in the house I heard Zombie scolding Nudie Nundie for locking us out. I could not hear Nudie Nudie's answer but my father Chief said to my mother, "Go easy on her, she was only protecting her virginity."

By Fourth Grade I had a nun for a teacher, Sister Francis. She was a no-nonsense but fair woman and she was also one of the nuns who insisted on the *Lake of Fire* penalty for stealing a pack of gum. That year I was introduced to tackle football with full uniform and cleated shoes. I loved it. I don't think we ever played any other team that first year but I do remember the scrimmages, the inter-team games. One boy, we called him Hugo, was not very big but he made up for his lack of size with sheer will and determination. Hugo would tackle kids twice his size and get them down. He would block anyone too. Over the years playing with him I saw him carried off twice with concussions. He was one tough Irishman.

I played right halfback on offense and left, outside linebacker on defense. I was not very good but loved the game. I remember when we were given our first uniforms, old but clean, hand-me-downs from past teams at our school. Everyone but me was issued the same color pants, a kind of gray, earth color. Mine, for reasons unknown, were bright red but fit fine. I decided that while I had a really different color of pants it simply did not matter. I thought the coach would only care what the guy in the red pants did on the field, nothing else. I was right. I kept mum and did not complain. Two or three weeks into the season our coach told me confidentially that he was happy with my efforts and handed me a brand new pair of football pants, the same color as everyone else. I never mentioned this to anyone because it was my private, little victory.

That first season playing tackle football we learned the basics, how to block, to tackle, to group tackle, some of the rules of the game and what attitude to take on pain. A lot of it was learning the vocabulary of football, what each position on offense and defense was named and what it was supposed to do. I remember the day we were introduced by our coach to a concept that has stayed with me ever since, the area on the football field relative to the offense, the flat. The flat? Where was this? We learned it and a bunch of other terms and how we switched direction on the field every quarter. For those who don't know, the flat is an area in the defense on the right and left sides about fifteen yards from the sidelines to the edge of the defensive line. The exercises were easy. Our coach did not make nine year olds work out endlessly in the warm Fall sun. Instead we had lots of fun scrimmaging, the white shirts versus the black shirts. Malbun always played quarterback and passed the football well. He loved sports and excelled at most of them.

Two simultaneous but opposite intellectual events happened to me during fourth grade. The first was, as a Catholic school boy, I was gradually but relentlessly indoctrinated into hardcore Catholicism. The Pope, I was taught, was all-knowing, infallible and omniscient in matters of faith and morals. This means that when any pope wrote an Encyclical touching on any aspect of Catholic faith or morals, he, like God Himself, could never be wrong. This seemed to be a strange and hard to believe doctrine and most of my peers accepted it but never mentioned it again. What kid our age even thought about it at all, other than in once a week religion classes with the nuns or priests? Making Water into Wine or the Virgin Birth were much more interesting items of Catholic faith to most of of my peers.

At the same time my parents had created five children of which I was the youngest, all of us avid readers. It started with the daily paper. I remember reading the Chicago Sun Times every day for most of my youth. My parents also subscribed to Time Magazine and Newsweek and we would read those magazines fervently. After we became official Catholics, my mother used to give us religious books at Christmas and birthdays. I remember one series I was given called Six O'Clock Saints by Joan Wyndham. These were books about various saints written for children. They did not touch on doctrinal affairs but concentrated on the real lives of the saints, making them alternately, warm, human, sometimes clumsy or preoccupied or frequently getting in trouble with their superiors or the state during their

30

lives. I think it remarkable that after six decades I still remember these books. They were the soft, warm side of Catholicism.

The second and opposite event was the result of my insatiable lust for books. By fourth grade I was riding my bike to the local public library to take out books almost daily. I remember many subjects of interest, sports, boys' adventures as in *The Hardy Boys* or *Tom Swift*, or Dave Dawson and Freddy Farmer winning every single battle of World War II. I also began to read about science and its heroes, particularly about Dr. Enrico Fermi, the famous nuclear physicist who, in 1942, deep underneath the stands at the University of Chicago's Stagg Field, built and successfully operated an atomic pile and created the world's first self-sustained nuclear chain reaction. When I read about this and noted he had done it a mere three years before my birth and within a few miles of my home, I knew he was my new supreme and local hero. This was not to mean I was no longer a fan of Mickey Mantle but Fermi and his record grew on me gradually as I grew older. It turned out he was not only a world-class physicist but he was a patriot and loved freedom. He thumbed his nose at the Fascist dictator Mussolini in the 30's and, when he was allowed by the Mussolini dictatorship to travel to Sweden with his family to receive the Nobel Prize, Fermi did not return to Fascist Italy but brought his family straight on to the United

States and never looked back. He was already a world famous physicist and America welcomed him; academia immediately employed him.

Inevitably these two very opposite idea systems Religion and Science were forming in my little brain. Catholicism with its emotional appeal to faith on one side; Science with its method requiring facts, evidence and a strict commitment to reason on the other. These polar opposites were to battle in me for several years before a major winner emerged.

Meanwhile my peers were interested in girls. At age nine I had no use for them and wondered why my friends dealt with them at all. After all, girls were weak, did not play sports, could not wrestle or run. They never appeared to climb trees. This was my attitude ... then. This was of course to make a 180 degree change in a matter of a year or so when strange and strong hormones began running thorough my system. It was to be the next year when my older brother Pendron told me about the physical differences between boys and girls. How interesting! My parents never gave us the Birds and Bees speech because they did something more influential and complete. They placed two detailed books on human anatomy and reproduction "hidden" in an old armoire of my mother's where we would never find them. I'll get into the details of this later but by leaving these books where they did, my parents' assured that I never went through a period where my knowledge of sex was learned in bits and pieces from my peers and older boys. No, I learned the names and functions of human sexuality right from the start.

I noticed that many of the boys in my class were followers and would go with and approve of any boy who chose to lead them. From the very beginning I thought this was pathetic, where were their minds and pride? My oldest brother Bruno remembers our parents' consistently rejected our pleas to do something "because everyone else was doing it." Each of us must have a true moral yardstick. Also, the weak ones would go along with one leader on Monday and sometimes by Wednesday, that leader was overlooked for a new one. They formed little cliques which came and went with great regularity. I thought it bewildering and kept my own counsel. From the very beginning I wanted to neither rule other kids nor be ruled by them. This intense individualism in me I think might have been almost completely innate because as I grew up, it remained and grew in me, including the choice of my personal politics, ethics and philosophy. Each of these values for me would be carefully chosen for a long list of consistent reasons.

Fourth grade had one harbinger of future change. Malbun and I were ice skating at a local rink one day in January. We met two girls our age from nearby Lincoln Middle School. I don't remember both of their names but I shall always remember the good -looking one. Her name was Jane Montgomery and she had curly, dirty-blond hair, a gorgeous smile. I thought she was the cutest human on earth. I don't know what we talked about but while we were in the warming house with our coats off but for one reason or another she touched my left arm with her hand, just for a second or two. Her hand was warm and that warmth seemed to flow upwards directly to my very being.

Her touch at that early age was not sexual in any sense. It was just very special and feminine. I was smitten and Malbun told me I was a basket-case for several days afterwards. But this was to be the first of many one-way romances. She went to Lincoln, a government school, I to St. Barnabas, rarely the twain would meet. Five years later I would go to the government high school in my town and Jane would be there too. By the age of 14 she had developed into a very attractive and curvaceous young woman but for reasons long-forgotten we never got together. Stand by for an incident which happened that included Jane Montgomery when we were juniors at age 16. I'll get there in a few chapters.

It was about this time Zombie decided that we children needed to take One-a-Day pills for extra nutrition. Each morning there would be a pill in front of my plate. For some vague reason I felt pills were somehow artificial and dangerous and that we ought to get our nutrition from our food. About two years later Zombie was cleaning out the centerpiece, a large, rectangular, ceramic container of fake, plastic flowers. She found all the pills I had rejected and hid in the centerpiece. 60 years later I still don't like excessive pill taking.

# Chapter Three Sex, Drugs, Rock and Roll

The summer before fifth grade I was old enough to start earning money mowing lawns. I had one customer who lived in the next block who owned an old reel-style power mower, with a Briggs & Stratton motor on the top. I would wind the starting rope around the starter reel and pull it vigorously. It would usually start on the first pull. At first I thought it was cool to be able to simply walk behind a machine that was doing all the major work. At home we had a push mower which had *me as the motor.* But as I did it week after week in the hot, humid summer sun, the novelty of a power mower wore off and it was just boring, physical work for a nine year old.

It was assumed by my "P's" (Parents) that I would save most of my 75 cents an hour from lawn mowing in the bank "for my college education." I did this religiously. I placed most of it in the bank (usually 90%). Along with the earning of many lawns and winter snow shoveling I found that when the time came, nine years later, I was able to pay for a flight course at the University of Illinois in full from my own bank account.

After cutting lawns in the summer I would hit the beach. We had a summer gang of St. Barnabas boys co-mixed with any girls our age we could coax into joining us. I loved Lake Michigan. When I first started swimming in it age six, it was clean enough to drink and I did so regularly. I managed to snare a coveted summer life guard job when I was 17 at a local public beach; by then the lake was not so clean. As a nine year old I would arrive at the beach, unroll the cuffs of my blue jeans, green, fresh grass clippings would fall out. I would frequently swim in my jeans.

I learned not to swim in my jeans the hard way. I distinctly remember walking home from the beach in my wet blue jeans, drinking a quart bottle of Coke in the afternoon sun. The next day my butt started itching. I had acquired a rash. My brothers immediately started making fun of me for getting "jock itch." and had to get some over-the-counter medicine to heal the rash. It was a simple case of ringworm; the medicine my father picked up at the drugstore for me I put on myself. It healed in several days and I never went home with wet clothes again. I made a point of drying off and putting on dry clothes before walking home.

By fifth grade our minds were bombarded with Catholicism but cracks were starting to widen. Suddenly girls looked different. Music became more profound. Sports were more involved and we finally had inter-school competition in football and basketball.

Let's begin with the girls. Along with what my brother Pendron taught me and the books my parents left in the armoire and hormones now rushing through my body, I began to see girls as very interesting propositions. For the first time in my life I finally understood, at least in a small way, why John Wayne in the movies stood on his horse next to a building, climbed up the side and entered the window where the good looking babe was. Then he spent a lot of time kissing her. What had seemed silly and a waste of time a mere year or so earlier posed an important question. What would *that* be like? Then there was Mary O'Sullivan, the girl who lived directly on my path to school. She was getting better and better looking and beginning to have curves and bumps in the most exciting places. Not big curves and bumps, but just a suggestion that she was going to get them.

The Catholic Church had an ongoing war with sex. It was to be done only between man and wife and even then only to procreate children. Worse, they inveighed against any form of what they called "self-abuse." which the sex book I had read called "masturbation." At first all this was just an abstract set of ideas battling against one another. But somewhere in my tenth year I discovered that this battle was very real and would affect me personally. The nuns and Catholic literature which they gave us said "self abuse" was a mortal sin. We would go to hell for eternity if we did it and died before we could go to confession.

Without making a huge deal of this I discovered one night how very, very exciting sex and masturbation were. I was thinking about girls and engaging them horizontally and found that my body reacted to these ideas. Blood rushed into my male part just as the book said it would. But the book had not informed me how pleasant it was. Then I found myself thrusting into my bedsheets and this was heavenly. Then it became unbearably good and I found myself undergoing a paroxysm of pleasure which, I later found out, my first "Big O." My male part spurted about a tablespoon of white fluid and I was all sticky. The pleasure in all this was indescribable.

For the rest of my youth and early life the battle lines were drawn. The pleasure of sex, even with myself, was terrific and the desire to share it with a girl was even more exciting. Opposed to this were the stern admonitions of the Catholics. Malbun and I discussed this and other similar problems we saw surfacing. How could this very brief but supreme pleasure which culminated in a short spurt or three of whitish fluid be wrong? Who did it hurt? My classmates and I compared notes. In this we were in total agreement. We all committed the sin of "self abuse." A lot. Daily, or more frequently, for most of us at that age.

Ben, the namer of things, came up with a description for all this. I called it the "Mort gage." The term combined mortal sin as in Mort with the word gauge, a measure of how frequently one engaged. This casual interchange about our boyish sexual pleasure continued through eighth grade.

When I explained it to my peers they all began to use the term as in, "What's your Mort gage today? "Answer...three, you?"

"Seven."

"Wow! You've been busy!"

Catholics had an answer for all this. It was called confession. We had to troop into church and, one by one, enter the confessional and tell a priest all our sins. At first it was embarrassing as all get out. I figured that the priest had heard it all many times and since it was dark on both sides of the screen, he probably did not even know which kid he was talking to. We had a list of typical sins for this age: Disrespecting our parents or teachers, using God's name in vain and of course the old Mortgage which we expressed as how many times we had masturbated. But even that word was not used. It was the sin of self abuse or "spilling the seed." The effort the Catholic teachers made to impart guilt upon us for this was heavy indeed. But it all came to naught. All through our youth we kept doing it and I finally decided the church was wrong. Maybe it was shortly after a priest in the confessional asked me if I had committed the *sin of abomination.*

"Abomination? I asked him, "What is that?"

"Laying with animals."

"No."

I was amazed. We lived in a suburb not a farm; there were no serious occasions to even be near an animal much less "lay with it." Why would he ask a ten year old boy such a ridiculous question? I am not exaggerating. This happened to me.

My ongoing reading had created a wide gap between what the nuns and priests were telling me and what the scientific method demanded. So I decided to go to the top to get it all straightened out. The "top" in this case, was the head of our local parish of Saint Barnabas, none other than the Right Reverend, Monsignor Allen Hilbert, then a towering figure of intellect, admired and (probably) feared by all for his intellectual sermons. My parents regarded him as a figure of national significance, I never found out why.

One day after school, I decided to go see to this towering figure and ask him to give me some proof for the existence of God. I walked over to the rectory, pushed the doorbell and waited. After a short time the woman who cleaned and cooked for the three priests who lived there came to the door. I told her I wanted to speak to Monsignor Hilbert if he could spare ten minutes for some questions. She disappeared and after minute or two there was The Great Man, smiling and inviting me to come in.

We went into his kitchen where he offered me cookies and milk which I happily accepted. We took these and went into his study. He asked me what was on my mind and I told him that I had been reading science and found that all the alleged "proofs" that my religion classes offered did not meet scientific standards of logic and proof. I told him that I had read Saint Thomas Aquinas' famous "proofs" and even these were not real proofs but only unbacked possibilities. Did he have some real proof for me?

The great intellect spoke some words that did not make sense and then said to me, "Ben you are a good boy from a fine family. Go home and take this entire matter to the Lord. Pray on it and you will find your way." In other words this famous priest, this towering intellect did not have a clue. Like all the others, he depended on faith, not reason. It was at this moment that Catholicism became an idea whose time had come and gone from me.

Which in some ways was too bad because I enjoyed many of the things we did as Catholics, the smell of incense, the great music, the pageantry, all my Irish friends. The three priests used to come over to our house for dinner occasionally.

43

When all three priests came together my parents called it a "Solemn High Dinner." Four years earlier, when the priests had dinner at our pad, I used to lay down on the rug next to the dinner table where my parents, older siblings and the three priests were sitting. The priests wore black shoes, black pants and black coats, a black shirt and a white collar that showed at the neck with a little rectangle. I would creep underneath the table and look at all these black pants and shiny, black shoes and wonder how they kept them so clean.

The all-important discussion with the great priest had let me down in terms of holding any respect for Catholicism or faith in general. I gradually moved more and more into a rationalist mode. This produced some odd consequences. We school boys and all the classes would leave the school at about 11 AM and walk the block to the church itself with the altar and choir boys peeling off midway to enter the door for their jobs. Since I was one or both at all times I guess the nuns were used to seeing me peel off for that door. This business of peeling off for the choir door became important in the next few years.

In the choir boy room where we put on our cassocks and surpluses to prepare to sing at mass, I had my first debate with Malbun on the issue of the existence of God.

44

Here we were, two ten-year-old choirboys sitting in our little costumes waiting to be summoned for our processional to enter the church. I told Malbun that I no longer believed in God at all because I saw no real proof. His answer was innocent but amazing. He, without ever reading philosophy or about Pascal's Wager, said, "Look Ben, why don't you spend your life claiming that you *do believe* in God? That way if He does exist you will go up to heaven with me. If He does not, it won't matter because heaven and hell might not exist either." My response was simple, "Don't you think God would know I was conning Him?" Malbun and I never resolved this debate over the next 55 years. We often came back to it but we never reached a conclusion. But we had a enjoyable time debating.

In fifth grade a new boy came to Saint Barnabas. We called him "Hickey" at first because of a bout of hiccups he had in our presence. But later I began to call him "Boy" as a mock term of derision. He began to call me Boy too and that's where it remains to this day. We are men in our 70's still calling each other "Boy." Boy, alternately with Malbun, experienced the next eight years with me as we cruised through the rest of Catholic grammar school and high school.

Boy was less athletic than Malbun but more sympathetic. Where Malbun was macho and stoic, Boy was thoughtful and interested in others. We got along famously. At different times the three of us, along with other friends such as Bar (I'll introduce Bar in another chapter.) and a few others, forged relationships of iron. Without ever going through a ""pinky swear" as in the film *Stand By Me*, we were loyal to each other and remained sincere for life. In Malbuns's case until the day he died. As we grew up we saw the other's lives, the gas his "P's" were always giving him and our desperate attempt to find girls and make out with them.

Due to the nature of Boy's parents' work, he moved from one suburb to another about five or six times in those eight years, almost always from one nice suburban home to another. We had a lot of fun in those places.

# Chapter Four  D-Nights, Cigarettes and the F-86

The summer before sixth grade was typical of a long, hot, humid Midwestern summer. We lived in a two-story home with three dormers, one of which, on the east side, facing the "Old Olsen's" home, was occupied by my brother Pendron and I. I lived in that home for 18 years, leaving it the last day of classes my senior year of high school. We had no air-conditioning so the nights were very uncomfortable lying there on the top of my sheets

sweating.


During most of my early years our room was last on the list for updating, so we had bare floors and bare walls of fading and pockmarked sheetrock. Upon these walls I would tape pictures of my heroes...Micky Mantle, Yogi Berra, the North American F-86 Sabre Jet, which I thought was the most beautiful airplane ever built. (I still do!), Dr. Enrico Fermi and Bill Bridgeman. You don't know Bill Bridgeman? He was a nationally known test pilot for Douglas Aircraft and broke speed and altitude records in the early 50's, at one time flying the Douglas Skyrocket to 1,250 miles per hour and later broke altitude records with the same plane. He was on the cover of the April 27, 1953 issue of Time magazine.

By the time we finally had the money to redo our room in about 1960, most of our walls were covered with Time Magazine covers of my favorite people. I wish I had had a camera to get a shot of it; one of my heroes, Dutch Kindleburger, head of North American Aviation, the firm that built the T-6 Texan, the B-25 Mitchell bomber, the most famous P-51 Mustang fighter that helped win WWII, the equally famous F-86 Sabre that won the air war over Korea in 1950 to 1953.

In that East facing dormer Pendron, who was two years older than me, taught me how to smoke. Where did he and I get cigarettes in the first place? Way too easily. Both of my parents smoked and so did my grandmother, although she had died by the timeI was in sixth grade Pendron, who was excellent at working with his hands, created a professional-looking cigarette box, made out of beautiful wood with a top with inlaid hinges, that he sanded and stained into a work of art. He gave it to

49

my mother. It was designed to hold a carton of cigarettes or ten packs. Pendron and I did not have to go far for cigarettes. We did not grab three or four packs at a time. We took one and smoked the 20 cigarettes in it very slowly so Zombie never missed them.

I started smoking at age ten. For the next 44 years I smoked regularly. It slowly and inevitably got me into a lot of trouble. This was presaged by observing both parents light up, smoke and extinguish cigarettes many times daily. I remember as a very young child, laying in my bed in the early morning. First I would hear Zombie's alarm clock going off and then the faint sounds of light, symphonic music coming from the Norman Ross Jr. Radio Show in Chicago.. Then I would hear a match strike and within a few minutes I could smell the sulfur and quickly after that the smell of tobacco.

In freshman year of high school I was seen smoking a block and a half from my school one afternoon after football season. The next Monday I was called into the athletic director's office and told to turn in the letter I had earned playing football. I was also barred from playing football sophomore year. At age 49 I had a heart attack which was highly attributed to smoking for the last 39 years. The problem was the physical problems came on so slowly I did not notice them until it was too late.

It was from the east facing dormer that I devised my exit from our home on many a night out with "da boys." It started that summer before sixth grade. Pendron and I slept with the windows open but the aluminum screen down to give us air. The screen could be raised and a second window would slide down to replace it for winter. We learned to manipulate these screens is such a way as to be able to raise and lower them quietly and easily from both inside and out. My parents never checked us out once we were asleep and quiet so....we both had a habit of quietly exiting our dormer, walking over the roof, down the west side, climbing onto a large tree. From there it was two or three practiced movements to the ground.

We called our nocturnal forays "D-nights." I guess it was because the Allies called June Sixth, 1944..."D-Day." We thought the "D" stood for the word Ditch. Who were we Ditching? Cops of course. Early on we decided that in order to not get caught on these all night forays, we made it a policy to avoid walking boldly down the center of the street and pay no attention to cars at 3 or 4 AM. Instead we walked along the sidewalks and whenever a car came we would fade into the brush and trees. We kept to this policy and in all the years of foraging around at night we were never once caught. Other kids were not so lucky. They tried it but got caught on the first night out.

What did we do on these "D-Nights?" Since it was usually warm and humid we almost always went pool-hopping and then the other big draw was some hen party we had heard about and tried to get into. I remember one night climbing onto the roof of a nice big suburban house to see into the window and talk to the girls inside. They were friendly but did not let us in. The next day I happened to drive by that house in a car and saw how really high I had gone. That was truly suicidal but I had not realized it because of the dark. I will relate more details of these all night adventures when I get into my high school years.

Sixth grade commenced and we played football, formed a team and once again I played right halfback and left outside linebacker. We even played Lincoln Middle School where Jane Montgomery went but I did not see her there that day. After the football games we would assemble, the "we" being my selected friends and an assortment of girls who lived near St. Barnabas, at one of the girl's homes to dance and socialize. That was where I invented a new dance, *The Hernia Hump*. It involved me lifting the girl high in the air and then spinning her around in my arms ending up with me getting a fake hernia. It only worked if the girl I lifted was reasonably thin.

About this time my parents announced that I was to go to dancing school at St. Barnabas on Saturday nights. I was terrified because I would have to wear a suit and tie and dance with girls I did not like or want to touch. On the Saturday night in question I informed my parents that I couldn't go because my tie was cut in half. They outsmarted me on that one. My father dug into his tie rack and gave me another which was not cut in half. I had to go.

When I got there I saw all my male Irish classmates looking as awkward and uncomfortable as me. Then the teachers, who were a dapper, married couple began to dance right smack in the middle of our group to some music on a record player. It was a waltz, in fact one of Johann Strauss, Jr 's best, *The Blue Danube*. ,...How did I know this? I had already fallen in love with the world of symphonic and opera music. This particular waltz was a major hit. My interest in dancing suddenly turned around as I watched this man and woman so expertly and gracefully glide about the floor.

They taught us the Waltz, Foxtrot, Cha-Cha and Jitterbug, ion the style of the mid 1950's. I found that I really enjoyed dancing with the instructor's wife because she was very good at making me feel in charge. I could see she enjoyed it too. Most of the girls in my class were average but I found one that was a really competent partner. Together we were the co-winners of a dance competition the class put on. I remember relaxing and enjoying the whole process. On the last night of the dance classes the instructor told us, "Remember this boys and girls, forget all the instructions we gave you. Boys, lead the girls and don't step on their feet. Girls, learn to follow and everything will come out beautifully in the end."

His words proved wise and gave me confidence. I loved to dance for the rest of my school days and beyond. Many girls told me they were happy to finally find a guy who knew how to lead and did so confidently. But there was another reason, well, two more reasons. The first was that I loved music and foxtrotting and waltzing were done to sometimes very glorious music which I deeply loved. The second reason was much more basic. To take a girl in your arms was to take her in your arms! It was a musical beginning to making out with her. Oh, did I mention? The girl I won the dancing contest with became a nun!

St. Barnabas not only had dancing classes but art and music as well. In art I was always trying to deliberately insert an air bubble into my bowls and other clay objects before they went into the kiln. This was because I was told that we should avoid this because an air bubble could make the clay to explode in the kiln. But try as I might, despite always carefully poking a hole in my clay and then filling most but not all of it. I never managed to blow up the kiln. When we were asked to make a work of art with clay I always tried make female nudes but these efforts were almost always ended with me crushing the whole thing when a nun entered the room and started to walk down the aisle looking at our masterpieces.

Music on the other hand was something I took seriously and loved. Father O'Donnelly taught us Gregorian Chant. The written music itself was different, the notes being square instead of round. This is because the monks, according to Father O'Donnelly, wishing to conserve ink and time, drew notes with a quill which gave off a distinct square if applied correctly. This is how normal notes as we would see them today look and next to it is an excerpt from an Introit in Gregorian scribe:

Father O'Donnelly was a very good musician and a good singer himself. Almost immediately he began to employ me to sing at weddings. It was easy! All we did was sing some of the normal mass, sometimes in unison, sometimes alternatively. The brides usually wanted us to sing Schubert's *Ave Maria*. This beautiful piece we would do tenor/baritone and we became pretty good at this too. We always sang it in

Latin. It was an enjoyable learning experience for me because by this time I wanted to sing grand opera like my hero Ezio Pinza did at the Met. Even better, I was usually paid $10.00 for the wedding gigs. At that age I was rich for a week!

We also had a lay teacher, Mr. Lehmann as a weekly music teacher. He was in our school a short time each day so we acted-out like crazed kids. When the music started I was all ears and eyes but otherwise I was as crazy as the rest. At that time most of us had Zippo lighters, the kind GI's in WWII had in the movies. They made a distinct clicking sound when you opened them right before striking them. We would all light them at the same time and place them on any horizontal surface around us. It grew quite strange in that music classroom.

At this time we also had miniature corncob pipes which we would occasionally place in our mouths. One day our nun grew tired of fifteen boys in her class all sucking on corncob pipes and went about confiscating them from us. All of them looked relatively new except mine which was brown and black in the bowl from heavy use. I would place tobacco from old cigarettes in the bowl and light it up with my Zippo.

A number of us who could carry a tune became choir boys. We wore black cassocks which was a kind of long, inner coat with buttons down the front in the middle. Over this went the white surplus and as I remember we had some kind of bow in the middle (but that part I'm weak on). We sang certain mass parts of the Introit, Kyrie, frequently the Gloria, Agnus Dei, and so on. These were sung in Latin when I grew up. Later they were sung in English. Then people could actually realize they were bowing down before a three part entity in the sky, confessing how sinful they were and throwing themselves on His mercy. I began to see it as hideous and degrading. And unless we were called upon to sing, I would ditch mass altogether.

I would peal off from the long lines of kids walking the block to the church from our school and go to the choir boy/altar boy entrance. From there I would roam about, sometimes investigating the "Catacombs," the long and poorly lit basement of the church which extended most of the way under the church to the back. This was reached by an old, rarely used door I discovered. Or sometime I would wait until the Mass had started and walk around and enter the back of the church, there to walk up the steps to the organ loft and from there climb a vertical, steel ladder to the inner roof of the church itself which one could walk along and look down a long string of openings where the ceiling lights could be accessed. On more than one occasion I would wiggle my fingers down to the lights and at a pre designated time, drop a tiny piece of paper so that my friends could see where I was. I did this many times in sixth, seventh and eighth grade and was never once caught at it or even asked about it. My inner beliefs were beginning to take the form of action. Where singing was involved I would play the part and sing up a storm but *underneath* my thoughts of rebellion were growing.

While the image of us singing as choirboys or playing about classrooms was on the innocent side we were not above acting grossly. My classmate Billy was the first to introduce us to the "instant bathroom." We often had to go to the bathroom but were nowhere near a toilet as we walked around our town. Billy solved that by hoping into a Cadillac parked on the street, defecating on the floor of the back seat and wiping himself on the edge of that back seat. Then he would calmly get out and rejoin us without batting an eye.

My contribution to this was to climb up a tree during our D-Nights and relieve myself from 20 or 30 feet in the air. For some reason Billy thought my impending bombardment as a kind of hysterical act of mirth. He would go nuts claiming that "Ben's about to Bomb!" Then when I did it he would shout out to all, "It's going to splat!" The rest of us thought that his behavior was very funny. Malbun made it a special shtick of his. 40 years later he would do his act, "Hey this is Billy calling the play-by play in "Ben's doing it from 20,000 feet!"

# Chapter Five The Cave and Brom Bones

Before I tell you about my adventures during seventh grade I want to reintroduce you to my father Chief and my sister Woban. Each a unique and interesting character on their own. My pop's name was David W. Archer and he grew up during the first decade of the 20th Century in Cincinnati, Ohio where his father was a judge. We called him Chief because he was always trying to convince us that we had a rich vein of Indian blood in us. As far as I know we had none. We are mainly French and German, not American Indian. He was always trying to get us to do Indian dancing and succeeded with Bruno and me. He was a big advocate of Boy Scouts, was also known to have demonstrated to his family the fine art of lighting farts on fire in great, long, blue jets to our massive laughter. He did his famous double fist pump which meant, "Forward, double time!" For the next five decades after grammar school, Malbun would always have me on the floor with laughter imitating Chief doing his famous fist pump.

I think Chief had no real desire to gain wealth. He had a steady job as an engineer, loved to play golf, had five kids and volunteered at local charities and the Boy Scouts. He was also a bit of a drunk, a habit which got worse and better and then worse as time went by. He was smart enough to not drink and drive so we saw the results of his over-drinking at home. He also had some funny sayings. My two favorites were "You get more with a spoon;" and he referred to women in the presence of his family, probably not in public, certainly not in front of the priests, as, Broadies. His parents were definitely Victorian as were my mother Zombie's. I remember one black and white picture of Chief standing outdoors beside a really old car and three rather stout women all dressed in long, billowy, black dresses with black hats. He was standing there, about 1913 in a WWI imitation uniform holding a long rifle at age nine. He was a competitive marksman in high school and went to the National Matches at Camp Perry. Ohio. There, he told me, he had a very high score going along with three straight bulls at the end. But when the scores were checked those last three bulls were on the target next to his so they counted as misses for him. Unfortunately, I did not know anything at all about my pop's adventures with rifle competition until I was 31 years old. Apparently his genes were in me as I became an avid shooter in Alaska at age 36, independently from my father.

My pop, being human, had both positive and negative traits. He was very handsome and looked a bit like William Holden. He played golf from April to late October so he had a constant tan on his face and arms all his life. But he was not *shaped* like Holden. Chief possessed a spherical belly that would, at times, rival Santa Claus. For this shape we frequently referred to him as "Sputnik."

My sister Woban was the classic middle child, always the mediator. She was the only girl among five children. As a result she was pampered and protected by all of us at various stages. We believed her to be the most beautiful girl in the world. Plus she was an excellent cook and frequently made fudge which she brought out of the kitchen in a large rectangular pan. She would cut the fudge into 16 or so little squares. But with five kids, two parents and two relatives all living in "The Shoe," her fudge rarely lasted for more than an hour before it was completely devoured by hungry Archers. I mentioned that we protected her but we also constantly maintained that she was to be our cook and fudge-maker for life. We would keep her in a tall tower like Rapunzel and never let her out. She also did not need protecting. When she was in seventh grade at St. Barnabas,. one of her classmates tried to grab her and kiss her against her will. I don't know whether it was a roundhouse or an uppercut but with one mighty swing she decked the guy but good. He never tried to kiss her again. Bruno called her "Bubba-sister." I called her Woban and that stuck.

Woban had a wonderful soprano singing voice and could remember lyrics easily. When she was in her freshman year at a local college she tried out for and won, the lead in Menotti's *Amahl and the Night Visitors*. She was also on the curvaceous side, so the lead in that show, a twelve-year-old boy named Amahl, might have been a stretch to play. Vocally she was perfect for the part. For over a month I helped her rehearse her part and in the process I learned the show over and over and loved it. We looked forward to the dress rehearsals but, one day, before they even started she was informed that, due to the fact that she was only a freshman, she would have to give up her leading role and let an older student do it. She was flabbergasted and crushed. I still, to this day, feel great resentment toward the music program at her college and the guy who made those decisions to remove her from her lead. Life was proving to be unfair in a very personal way.

About fifty years after her brilliant defense move against her aggressive classmate, a friend of my brother told me something about her. We Archers all thought Woban walked on air and was most beautiful. But, according to one of my brother's peers at St. Barnabas, two years younger than Woban, all the boys in his class would try to be close to the window in the gym when Woban's class was walking down the hall. Why? I asked him. He said that they all hoped to see Woban

65

walking along. She was a big hit with the boys and could have had any one she wanted.

In her earlier academic career, in about third or fourth grade, Woban wrote a story. It was about a rabbit but her rabbit was made famous in our family because she misspelled the word rabbit as "ridder!" My father picked this up and gently poked fun at her. Then we brothers chided in and whenever something bad was done at our house, we blamed it on the "ridder." This went on for her entire youth even through high school. If we were driving along and saw a rabbit, a loud chorus of "Hey there's Woban's ridder over there!" Finally we all just began to call all rabbits...ridders. When Woban married her long time boy friend after his graduation from Notre Dame, guess who sang at her wedding with Father O'Donnelly? Moi of course.

By the time seventh grade started I had grown taller and again played football on our team at St. Barnabas. We were now eligible to play with the older kids on our school's "varsity" team. I played left end. We now had clean, relatively new uniforms with our school colors and played a different, Catholic, grammar school almost every weekend. Oddly I don't remember how well we did but I remember enjoying it thoroughly.

In order to appreciate the next drama, I have to explain that my parents did not give me a weekly stipend like many of my friends received. Allowance was not in my vocabulary. I asked my mother about this. She told me I was provided with food, clothing and the necessary money to live pretty well and that the work I did on the garden or lawn was simply a chore which was expected of all children. The fact that other kids in my class had allowances, sometimes pretty hefty allowances, was irrelevant. All of this had an effect on me. If I needed money I had to work on lawns in the summer, rake leaves in the fall and shovel snow in the winter. If I did not have any work I walked around with no money at all on me. I therefore learned how to scrounge, acquire things by trading or, occasionally, not too often, by swiping them. So it was.

One of the benefits from this austere monetary policy was that I've been a penny-pincher ever since. I learned to go to the library if I wanted to know something or acquire a book. Most importantly, I observed, that the kids with money were no smarter, better looking or adroit on the football field or "got the girl" than those who were poor but clever or worked harder. In other words I was taught to understand the concept of merit and hence evolved a later political philosophy of meritocracy, as opposed to inherited wealth.

With this in mind, we seventh and eighth graders of St. Barnabas went on a combined field trip from the Chicago area via train to the capital of Illinois, Springfield, home of Abraham Lincoln. I was given a brown bag with a sandwich and an apple in it for my lunch by my mother. Both were consumed by 10 AM. We went to various government buildings and museums before we went to the highlight of the trip, a visit to an underground cave system. Boy, Bar, Malbun, Billy and I stuck together through this adventure. I still have a giant black and white photo of all the kids with the nuns standing there looking into the camera. It's amazing that I can remember many of their names from 60 years ago but can't remember what I had for dinner last night.

When we arrived at the large cave we began to walk down a broad entrance and before we went into any tunnels there was a large wishing-well type pool where people cast their pennies, dimes and quarters hoping for "good luck." I can't help but thinking now, after watching every single Star Trek in the Eighties, what Scottie the engineer had said once when he was left on the bridge in charge of the Enterprise. "Good Luck" he was told, as the Away Team left for the planet below. Scottie mumbled, "Luck, hell, I'll trust to a full phaser bank." I never saw any evidence that luck was a guarantee of success. Besides, I had no money to literally throw away into a pool and everyone there *knew* I had no money. So while my peers were throwing coins into the pool I stood there and watched. Finally, I decided to have some fun. I made a big act out of getting ready to throwing in a coin. I wound up, I paused, I looked around, yes, I had most of the class' attention, wound up again and threw my "coin" into the pool. Except my "coin" floated on the surface of the pool. It was not a coin but a match I had taken from a pack in my pocket. A huge collective groan went up from the crowd. I'm still laughing more than 60 years later.

The next memorable exploit in seventh grade was the "Brom Bones Incident." Just as the four boys in *Stand By Me* were lured to the woods to find the body of a boy killed by a train, we as twelve year olds were lured to find the body of woman killed by a local commuter train. We heard about it in the morning. After eating our lunches, instead of heading to the nearby park for a game of softball or football, we all rushed down to the railroad tracks to see if we could find the body. The railroad tracks were in a recess as they went through our town. The tracks were about fifty feet lower than the surrounding area so bridges served for the main streets to cross the tracks. We boys knew every means of getting down to the area where we heard the woman was killed.

We looked and looked but saw not one eye, leg, or head. We came up completely empty before we heard that a cop was coming and we ran in all directions to evade him. Later, that afternoon, as we sat in our classroom, we heard an announcement that all the seventh grade boys were told to come to the school library...no reason given. When we got there, a rather large, over-weight, red-faced cop was there. He began to lecture us rather sternly about how dangerous the tracks were and how foolish our attempt to find the body was and that we were obviously the most im-moral boys on earth, on and on and on. I resented this because we had not hurt any-one; we did not get caught and how dare this rather ugly man berate us? So I stood up and asked him if he had any specific reason to speak to us? Was he charging any of us with a crime? And if not why should we have to sit there and listen to him if we were innocent? As I fully felt we were. In essence, all we had done was trek around the tracks for a while, touching nothing and disturbing no one.

The nun in charge came up to me, slapped me a good one across my face. The noise of that slap was rather loud. I remember the noise of her slap more than the physical effect of it. But I had made my point. The big cop looked flabbergasted and eventually clomped out the door. I've forgotten what the nun said to me directly after the slap or what she said to all of us later but I do remember the resulting effect it had on my popularity. I was suddenly the class champion. I immediately named the cop "Brom Bones" from the novel *Legend of Sleepy Hollow* by Washington Irving. Brom Bones was a loser, a bully and I never liked him, apparently not an untypical reaction to him. The rest of the seventh grade boys pretty much felt the same way I did and we banded together to gain our revenge upon him.

Several months later we were playing a game of pickup softball in the park near the school when we saw Brom Bones' police cruiser slowly drive by. We watched him park the car and go into a nearby restaurant. This is when we struck. Stationing one of us directly across from the entrance to the restaurant to signal us if Brom Bones should come out, we went to his squad car and found he had left it unlocked. It was the habit of cops then (in the Fifties) to have a big shot-gun stuck in a brace which held it in a vertical position with the muzzle upwards about a foot from the cop's head as he drove along. Did we steal that shot-gun? No, no, no, we did something much better. Billy had a rubber, a prophylactic, which he produced and offered for our Revenge. . One of us opened the package and placed the prophylactic over the top of the muzzle and pulled it down as far as it would go. We then beat it out of there and reassembled in the park.

Eventually, as Brom Bones came plodding out of the restaurant, all our eyes were upon him. We were sitting around on benches in the park and managed to look more innocent than choir-boys at Mass. He got into his car, started it up and then turned it off and came storming out. He started to walk directly at us but began to slow down as his tiny mind in his massive head finally got around to telling him he had no real evidence that we had   placed the prophylactic on his gun. He slowed down and the look on his face of utter confusion and defeat made our victory all the sweeter. You *can* fight City Hall! At least a little, now and then.

It was at the tender age of twelve when my penchant for writing things began to blossom ever so gently. There was a column in the Chicago Sun Times that consisted of people writing in with questions which the Sun Times would then ask people on the street. I wrote in with the question, "Do you have any trouble getting your children to take baths?" If your question was used, they would send you a check for something like $5.00. I forgot about it but about three weeks later my question appeared in print and I duly received the $5.00. My first venture into print for money!

I noticed that Chicago Helicopter Airways ran a twice daily flight from our suburb to O'Hare Field and Midway Airport. In fact I lived on the very road which the chopper landed. It was a Sikorsky S-58 model and was most graceful as it came in for a landing, smoothly touched down with a tiny little bounce and disgorged its passengers. I wrote a letter to the management of Chicago Helicopter Airways telling them how much I admired their helicopter which landed on a helipad exactly 1.1 miles west of my home and wanted to know all about it.

They wrote me back and invited me to ride the helicopter from my suburb to O'Hare and on to Midway where they had their headquarters. They invited me but they did not offer *to pay* for the ride. I was so thrilled to actually fly in the first place that I took $17.50 out of my bank account, with the full approval of my P's, and bought the ride on the chopper. It was my very first flight and I was super-thrilled. I think the company executives were mind blown when a twelve-year-old boy exited the chopper at Midway. Six years later, at the University of Illinois, flying from the airfield at Champaign-Urbana, I soloed a 7FC Tri-Champ, a pilot at last.

In seventh grade my opposition to the alleged existence of God, my ongoing battle with being expected to believe in miracles, in one man being actually three and creating a situation where a virgin woman gave birth to a child, the father of whom was also himself and that we would eat this man's flesh at Mass in the form of a communion wafer, a circular piece of unleavened bread which was supposed to be his actual flesh once the priest had mumbled over it?*

I began to slowly build up a resentment at this whole untenable theology. However I kept peace with my Irish friends and the teachers, letting only my inner circle know of my atheism. My attitude at the time was, more or less: You can believe in these silly ideas, I will need a bit of proof and logic to believe anything. It seemed at the time to be a mere personal choice like preferring chocolate to vanilla ice cream. This tolerant notion of mine slowly and incrementally changed as I read more and learned more of the world, especially of the constant and bloody religious wars that occurred in the Fifties and to this day killing people by the millions over the globe.

*The priests *did* mumble because they said this phrase over and over: "Hoc est enim Corpus meum." (This is my body.) Catholicism professes that when the priest consecrates the bread and wine, it becomes the body and blood of Christ in the miracle of transubstantiation. Never mind the question of cannibalism, how could this wafer be His actual body and at the same time only *represent* His body? This is the stuff of the "how many angels can fit on the head of a pin" debate. I found that as I learned more and more of the inner ideas of the church, that they were of this kind, totally useless and untestable.

My old man had a motto regarding food. *Quantity Not Quality*! This might have sprung from the fact that he was paying the food bill for five, very hungry kids, two parents and for the first part of my childhood, an aunt and a grandmother... nine people in all. Nick the Borden's Milkman would bring us literally gallons of milk twice a week. I remember the gallon milk bottles in our refrigerator. We had a bread man come to our home regularly whose truck smelled so wonderfully of bread, rolls, cupcakes and all sorts of good stuff.

In fifth grade I remember a popular song called "Standing on the corner" written by Frank Loesser but popularized by the The Four Lads, which had a line,

*"Saturday and I'm so broke. Couldn't buy a girl, a nickel Coke..."\**

We knew many places that had nickel Coke machines. The kind that had Coke bottles all lined up horizontally and when you put your nickel in the slot, you could extract one coke bottle from this line. My problem was that most of the time while I was at school I had no money. Money came from working on gardens and lawns in the summer, raking leaves in the fall and shoveling sidewalks in the winter. Between these jobs which were not that easy to find, I had no money, so a nickel Coke was usually a dream to me.

Our food at home was on the whole very good. But Zombie used to complain that her brood of five kids and her husband refused to eat anything but "hamburgers and hot dogs." This was an exaggeration but she maintained it. Our weekly menu was dominated by having specific things to eat on different days of the week. Friday night was some form of tuna fish because we were Catholics. Saturday night was frequently hot dogs. Sunday? A large ham nicely cooked for nine people. Monday through Thursday it might vary between casseroles, a roast of some kind or, infrequently, Chinese food. I did not like my mother's effort at Chinese. I did not recover from that early dislike until I was in the Army in Honolulu, Hawaii and had *real* Chinese food and began to love it.

Zombie had everyone involved in the whole meal production. My sister Woban was her assistant cook. The two oldest brothers Bruno and Aubere, were waiters. All four of the oldest kids washed and dried the dishes. Bruno, stationed in the pantry, caught China-ware dishes flung to ham and stacked them on shelves. After enough misses to provoke Zombie's wrath, she bought plastic plates. As the youngest, I was given the least to do. Eventually my regular job was to take out our old, ball-shaped, Hoover vacuum cleaner and suck up all the crud we had dropped on the floor during the meals.

During those meals Chief would sit on one end of the large dining room table, Zombie would sit on the other end. Bruno and Aubere would sit on the side closest to the kitchen so they could get up and down to act as waiters. Interesting, at the end of most meals, if you looked down at our table from above it would look like some giant magnet had been placed below pulling all the dishes into polar arrangement with one large group of dishes in front of Bruno and the other in front of me. I guess we had huge appetites.

For desserts, Bruno would take orders of *how much* if we had ice-cream. With most of the kids he knew that if we had any real choice in the matter we would simply take as much as we could so he would dole out an equal amount to each of us. For my grandmother Nudie Nundie, he would ask her how much ice cream she wanted and she would always reply, "Oh just a small taste." He would present her with her bowl first since she was the oldest at the table. Her bowl would be most of a pint of ice cream. Then he and Aubere begin serving the rest of us. By the time I got my bowl, Nudie Nundie had finished her huge bowl and would discreetly push it aside.

It was at these meals and all through growing up that we kids learned how to do fractions…with a vengeance. There were five kids and Chief would bring home a six pack of 12 ounce Pepsi's in bottles. That is when I learned what a fifth of something was. That was when I learned not to trust the person who did the dividing. We created the fast rule, *He who divides can not choose*. I did not know the notation 1/5 but I sure understood its meaning. This is also when we began to barter and trade off food for other food, food for toys, food for first grabs at other things. This was all part of growing up in the Fifties among my siblings.

Well, while most families had their favorite desserts, my old man's motto of *Quantity not quality* paid off. By the time I was ten or so, instead of all this dividing and choosing, my father devised a magnificent and efficient method of making sure we all had the exact same amount. We had plenty of large carafes in our kitchen, usually made out of steel. Chief came up with the "QT-PT!!," pronounced flagon Tee Pee Tee. He had five kids to deal with, all hungry, all eager to see that he or she was not cheated by the others. He henceforth would bring home five quarts of root beer and five pints of vanilla ice cream. Thus each child would take his quart and pint (Thus the QT-PT) and dump them into a large flagon and make a giant "Black Cow," a full quart of root beer and a full pint of ice cream. These we would consume with great speed and happiness.

RG, who would eventually marry my sister Woban, when seeing all five of us, including his then girlfriend, consuming these truly Gargantuan desserts, did a very funny bit. When playing charades, he would roll on the floor and make pig-like

79

noises. We had no idea what this meant until he finally let us know it was the five Archers consuming QT-PTs.

*If you want to hear the song *Standing on the corner.*" here is a link to YouTube with a great rendition of it:    https://www.youtube.com/watch?v=bNA6ilPK-bo

# Chapter 6  The Top of The Heap

The summer before eighth grade was a wild and busy time. I had grown taller and was able to caddy at the local golf course.  It was hard work, especially when I caddied double, as in carrying two golfer's bags around 18 holes of golf.  I was usually paid four dollars per round for one golfer  so doubling up netted me  eight bucks usually with a tip of $2.00 and a coke thrown in at the end. In 1958 this was a king's ransom to me. While I did this many times I never grew to like it.  I observed that regardless of the occupation, age, relative wealth or any other factors, the men I caddied for almost always ended up by the fourth hole on, talking about women and sex, which was the major topic of all my male friends' and me at age twelve. Come to think of it, it still is.

During this summer  I answered the phone at home one early afternoon. It was my father calling. I answered with a normal, "Hello." He said, "Hi," and then paused. He had an incredibly warm baritone voice and I heard in his simple "Hi," a string of warmth coming-out. His "Hi" said, "I acknowledge you my son, I am aware of you and enjoy your presence. " Then he told me to tell my mom that he was working a job in Rockford and would be late getting home, maybe seven or eight PM. He thanked me and hung up. I told my mom and then went to the local golf course to meet Malbun.

It happened that I had arranged to meet Malbun at the local golf course that day. As I pedaled in on my bike I saw my father taking his golf bag out of his car and walking toward the first hole. He was definitely not working a job in Rockford, Illinois; he was going to play 18 holes of golf. He had lied to me and mom. I casually rode my bike up to where he was and smiled a greeting at him, thinking that I had caught him in *the great lie* and would be able to blackmail him in some fashion. But he did not bat an eye, nor look embarrassed in any way. I guess he was a better actor than I thought. Anyway, that was that. I never was able to capitalize on catching him cleanly in his *great lie.*

As long as we are on the subject of my father…he was not an ogre. In fact he had a number of wonderful virtues. As long as I can remember he would frequently take us, all five kids, to see double features at the local cinema. After WWII there was a never ending avalanche of war movies, mostly starring John Wayne. Dad took us to all of them. In 1958 alone we saw my all time favorite jet, the F-86, featured in *The Hunters,* with Robert Mitchum and a young Robert Wagner. We saw the incredibly beautiful *South Pacific* starring Rossano Brazzi as Emile de Becque and Mitzi Gaynor as Nellie Forbush the nurse. Brazzi could not sing a note but excellently lip-synced his singing parts to the powerful voice of opera star Giorgio Tozzi. This movie gives me tears to this day. We went to *No time for Sergeants, Run Silent, Run Deep* with Burt Lancaster and Clark Gable. He even took us to see *The Blob*, starring Steve McQueen which did not scare me a bit because the monster looked like a delicious bowl of cherry Jello.

I think I was highly brain-washed by all the WWII movies I was taken to during my early development. The essence of this brain washing seemed to be: The US was not only victorious but conducted war in a most dignified manner. All Germans were Nazis, cunning and very bright but vile murderers. All Japanese were "gooks" and total scum. This was the net message to my young brain at the time. I don't know how it affected my siblings but I remember my sister Woban, as late as the

90's, calling out from the back seat of the car we were riding in, "Bandits on stern! Closing!"

The summer of 1958 I continued to expand the number of lawns I mowed every week. I placed an ad in the local paper and got a lot of business from it. I got one call from a lady who lived about three miles north of us who told me she would come and get me and take me back after I cut her lawn. Her lawn was more like a small clearing in a jungle of various growth. All she had to cut it with was an old, rusty, push mower. I told her I would have to oil and get the old mower going before I actually cut her lawn. She provided some oil and rags. I carefully cleaned it and oiled it and tried it out. It worked fine after my cleaning. I cut a small open area about 50 feet wide by ten deep, a little rectangle of green lawn among the jungle plants. She was delighted with this and took me home paying me an extra dollar tip and asking me to come again next week.

I cut her lawn regularly for the next four years, gradually increasing the amount of grass area against the jungle. She also had one of those old homes that had a roof covered with growing things. I cut that back too. Plus she had a pink, convertible Chevy which she allowed me to take on dates in my junior and senior year of high school.

We had a greater number of D-nights that summer before eighth grade than ever. We hopped pools, swam in Lake Michigan and went over to girl's homes who were sleeping on their porches. One night I tried to orchestrate an *Unknown Trinity* at one girl's home. I was going with her. The plan was for me to come over one night when she was sleeping on her porch. We would be making out on the porch cot and I would ask her if she could get me some water from her kitchen. When she went into her house to get the water I would sneak Boy and Bar into the porch and hide them underneath the cot where they could witness any success, or lack of it, I would have with the girl. As things turned out they began laughing before I got anywhere with the girl so she discovered their presence. To her credit she laughed as hard as we did over the whole situation. Try as I might I can not remember her name.

By eighth grade I was over 5'8" and still growing. I had absorbed most of the liturgical music the Catholics are so expressive with and wanted more than ever to be a professional opera singer. My second oldest brother Aubere, five years older than me, went through Lakeside High School Music Department and had won several starring roles in the light operas they put on. He was Fred in *Oklahom*a, sang in *Carousel* and played the preacher in *Down in the Valley*. I wanted to do the same and observed the musical world very closely as my time would come soon.

Aubere and I had a special relationship. When I was five years old, he completely dominated me in most respects. Don't all big brothers? Isn't that their job? He would alternately pound me and reward me. Often he would come up to me and the first thing I felt was a hard hit on my shoulder or back. After a while I got so tired of being stuck by this monster that I would lie on the floor knowing he would not bother to bend over so low as to be able to hit me with his fist or kick me. He had me literally punch drunk. But then the next day he would place me on the handlebars of his bike and pedal me to downtown to Walgreen's and buy me a "Shake-a-Plenty," a milkshake which cost 27 cents and used real strawberry ice cream .

He was a typical big brother in terms of taunting me and attempting to terrify me. At six in 1951, my pop took us all to see a black and white movie called *The Thing*, starring Kenneth Toby and James Arness as the monster. In the movie, a professor, sitting at a microscope, was analyzing the evidence the monster had left behind,. He characterized the monster as "...essentially plant-based, a carrot." It truly terrified me.

Later at home, I mentioned to my brother Pendron that I thought the "Carrot People with orange hair" might live in our basement. I was extremely reluctant to go down into our basement during the night after that. Aubere overheard me tell Pendron about my fear of the "Carrot People." He then took the time to suggest most carefully that while he did not know for sure *if* the Carrot People did exist in our basement, then again they might, and I ought to be careful going down there. Later I was down in the basement at night with the lights on but someone (Guess who that might be?) turned out the lights and I was a utterly terrified six-year-old in a very dark basement with the Carrot People! Eventually I got out of there without the Carrot People getting me.  I think I got another ride to Walgreens after that and consumed another, wonderful, strawberry "Shake-a-Plenty." At that time my brother Aubere was cutting lawns so he could afford to pay for such an expensive reward..

With the "Carrot People" long forgotten by eighth grade, I was appointed by Mr Lehmann, our music teacher, to portray the role of a priest. I sang the latin exchanges with the chorus and portrayed a number of the well-known rituals of the Catholic Mass at a musical event at our school. I may have become a convinced atheist by this time but this was a singing gig, so it took precedence over my mostly hidden atheism.

The part required that I wear all the priestly vestments, hold the chalice, turn to the audience, which consisted of the rest of the school underclassmen and invited parents and sing the priest's part at the mass. Most importantly I acted the part of the "Transubstantiation" where the priest takes an oversized, circular piece of white, unleavened bread, lifts it above his head and holds it there in a dramatic gesture and intones, "Hoc est enim Corpus Meum." This act is supposed, by Catholic doctrine, to change the bread into the actual body of Jesus Christ. No one my age ever asked, "Are we now cannibals by doing this?" So here I am, a 13 year old, singing the part of a priest doing this alleged creation of a man's body out of a piece

88

of bread. As Boy told me later, you made the old ladies cry when you did that and you got to eat the large wafer! Oh my singing career was looking up. I was paid in unleavened bread.

But Ben Archer, the oh-so innocent boy, singing the part of the priest that made the old ladies cry, was in many ways a typical youth. I rarely had money in my pocket so I on occasion was not above nipping some if I had the chance. As altar boys we would grab the hosts if we could get out hands on them and eat them. They melted in the mouth. But on one occasion Malbun and I were asked to assist the ushers after a church service by each taking several of the money baskets with envelopes filled with cash and checks which constituted the offerings of that particular mass from a place near the altar, though a narrow passage to the place where the priests and altar boys put on their vestments. I walked slightly ahead of Malbun and noticed that there were a number of pieces of green money, fives and tens, even a twenty or two, sitting in the wicker basket one foot from my hands. Looking around me to see if any adults were present and finding them nowhere to be seen, I grabbed several of the tens and a five or two. Malbun observed the whole thing.

Later when we were out of our altar boy costumes and away from the church. Malbun asked, "How much did you get?" I reached into my pocket and found two fives and two tens, making the haul an even thirty bucks which to me was a great bonanza. That was the only time I ever stole something from the church. Malbun no doubt shared some of the loot with me by allowing me to buy him food at a nearby restaurant. He never squealed. He took that particular secret of ours to his grave.

Malbun taught me lessons in manners and tolerance through his actions over the first six years I knew him. I noted that he never called people names. He would get highly irate when other boys did, especially when boys used the phrase "Spaz" to deride somebody who was awkward or uncoordinated. In fact he would stand up to anyone who did so, even older boys who were much bigger. I quickly learned why. His sister Joy, had Cerebral Palsy. I mentioned earlier that when I first met her she terrified me. Now I will say why. She was awkward, spasmodic; she drooled excessively and her speech sounded to me, at age eight, like a monster, at least when I first met her. As we evolved from third to eighth graders, I spent many many hours at Malbun's pad and gradually began not only to lose my fear of Joy, but learned to understand her. She could communicate clearly if the person speaking to her was patient.

Malbun did something else for me too. Around this time most of the boys started to use foul language, the terms shitty, bastard and mostly the term fuck, fucked up or fucker. As as a boy highly interested in speech, oratory and operatic delivery I was not immune to using these words. Gradually we were all using them in every sentence on the playground, but not in the classroom. I noticed this dichotomy and thought about it and came to the conclusion that these words were verbal crutches. I told myself that I would no longer use them at all. But I was already hooked. So I told Malbun, who was a very muscular and powerful guy, that he could strike me about the shoulder or arms one hard blow, every time I used the term fuck or any derivative. (How hard? As hard as he wanted!) And I would not strike him back. Malbun fairly leaped at this offer and within two minutes of making this pact, his strong arms were pummeling me with enthusiasm. I learned to completely eviscerate that word and its derivatives from my active vocabulary by about dinner of the next day, my arms becoming slightly black and blue. Today we would call Malbun's hitting me every time he heard me speak the forbidden word as "positive feedback." Whatever it's called it hurt like hell, but it worked.

Both my parents smoked prodigiously all their lives. Even toward the end they continued, relenting only by smoking filtered cigarettes, instead of Camels or Chesterfields which were *full monte*. One summer early evening I distinctly remember a shaft of sun coming through the window and shooting past my mother as she sat sitting on the edge of the couch smoking one of her many cigarettes. Malbun and I sat next to her. We engaged in some casual conversation but our real purpose was to count how many exhalations after taking in a full drag of smoke she would exhale with smoke still in them. The ray of sun gave us a perfect backdrop to see the less dense exhales.

The first exhale was, as to be expected, a full-blown waft of smoke. As we continued speaking to her we counted, #2 almost as much smoke in it as #1. #3, still somewhat cloudy. By her 4th exhale, Malbun was looking amazed. Her #5 contained easily-seen amounts of smoke, so easy that the sun ray was not necessary. #'s 6 through #10, while diminishing in smoke, we could still see it easily. #11 it became necessary to see it through the sun ray,  but we could *still* see each exhalation still had smoke in it. We were counting and seeing smoke come out by #17 when she took a new drag! While we thought this was comical at age 14, just over a decade later in 1972, Zombie died of smoke related lung problems, emphysema to be exact. I flew in from Hawaii, my home at the time and arrived at her hospital bedside to see and hear her gasping for breath under a transparent plastic tent, still holding in her hand a non-existent cigarette and periodically tapping off nonexistent ashes. Those death gasps still haunt me to this day. Later, at the wake, Bruno remembers his son Louis A. and he standing by the open casket. Up walked a man smoking a cigarette. Louis A. screamed at him, "Don't do that!"

Looking at our behavior as 13 year olds in eighth grade I remember that we could be cruel but not overtly or intentionally. For example. there was one girl who was an early- bloomer and wore straight skirts which revealed her very attractive figure. Boy told me he really liked how she wiggled and his eyes were bought down to the that part of her we all so wanted to investigate. I thought this over and the next time I saw her, sure enough, she was wearing a seductive straight skirt. The word clitoris suddenly popped into my mind.  I immediately gave her a nickname, Jan the Cleat. Not to be misunderstood,  the term cleat was a football cleat, a pointy thing on the bottom of football shoes. Her nickname did not refer to a football cleat. Instead she was most attractive in this general area of her anatomy.

The rest of the boys picked that nickname up like a firestorm. Within a day or two of making up this nickname up, one of my peers came up to me and asked me if I had seen Jan the Cleat. More interestingly, the girls themselves somehow got wind of this nickname and on several occasions asked me if I knew she had that nickname. I answered that a gentleman never tells, a line I had heard in a movie. The only question that remains unanswered is, did Jan the Cleat ever hear herself called this? Would she have understood that it was, in a crude, boyish way, a compliment? I think so because the girls picked up on it with great haste. They seemed to know exactly what we had in mind. And never complained.

On the other hand there was a girl at our school who was slightly overweight, had short, frizzy hair. As she developed, instead of nice curves, she became a classic Sherman tank. Plus her face was reminiscent of the Russian, female tractor driver on Commie posters of the 50's. She was, to put it plainly and honestly, ugly. We called her Sally D. The boys all knew that whenever one asked if so and so was a Sally D, she was well worth avoiding. Were we acting insensitively? Were we turning a girl into her looks alone instead of her "personality?" I don't think so. Humans of both sexes prefer beauty to ugliness. We were being honest. Have you ever been offered a blind date and when you asked what does she look like, you get, "Well, she's got a good personality." Then you know you were about to be planted with a Sally D. Don't believe me? Great literature confirms it. Read the *Hunchback of Notre Dame* or *Phantom of the Opera* and tell me ugliness is a good thing. In these classics, the monsters may have finally got the girls to value them, we had to put up with their looks the entire book or movie.

By eighth grade most of us had won the Battle of the Fingernails. What is *that* you ask? My mother Zombie had given her four Archer boys a good, basic course in personal hygiene. We all endured the "Saturday Night Bath." How many times did I sit in a large, warm bathtub with my brother Pendron and simply play in in the tub as a five-year-old? Since we began the bath covered in dirt from playing all day in it, the surface of the tub quickly began to look pretty bad and we would push it toward each other with the phrase, "All the crud to your side!" My mother would comment afterwards if we had not cleaned our fingernails to her standards.

I noticed that my older brothers, Bruno and Aubere, always seem to have perfectly clean, well-groomed fingernails while I had a major time keeping mine clean. The battle was to get your fingernails clean and keep them that way. But, as a very busy kid, playing in the dirt, throwing dirt, climbing trees, eating anything I could grab with my hands, wrestling with my brothers and other kids, I was always dirty or so it seemed. How could I ever win the Battle of the Fingernails?

I watched my oldest brother Bruno. He seemed to have won the Battle for good. His fingernails were always clean. I noticed that he would frequently go to the john, clean his hands with a quick wash with soap and water, dry off and go back to whatever he was doing. After a few months of experimentation I was well on my way to learning the secret of how to keep your fingernails clean most of the time. The secret was......to not get them dirty in the first place or, if you did, quickly go to the john and clean them. By third grade I had mastered this secret.

During this time that I went to Catholic Mass every day with my classmates. We boys would stand in a line in a pew. We would stand, sit or kneel, as the Mass required. As we stood our hands would frequently be on the top of the pew in front of us, so I was almost forced to observe my classmates' hands and their fingernails. A good 2/3 of the boys in my class had filthy fingernails which I looked down upon with great distaste. Each year of the six I went to St. Barnabas that number moved toward 90% being clean. By eighth grade there was only one major holdout who seemed to be oblivious to personal grooming. His fingernails remained filthy into the second half of sophomore year in high school. The other 9 percent who had not won The Battle by eighth grade were marginal, sometimes coming in as clean, sometimes not. Boy, my friend for life, who joined us in fifth grade, won the battle at the very first. Malbun was close behind him. Oddly, there was one guy in high school, a rich kid even, who never learned to win the battle and 100% of the time had terrible grooming.

Why do I even bother to write about this? Because cleanliness and grooming paid off for me big time with the girls. One girl told me her mother liked me. Really? Yep. Why? She said you were the cleanest boy I had ever gone out with. You appeared one evening right after work with old, faded pants but you had taken the time to put tape over the holes (I worked at a factory that manufactured tape!!) and your hands were very clean. She became a very close GF. I will write more of her later. Besides the advantages with girls, cleanliness was to me the absolute first thing to battle disease. I had seen and read of the germ theory and one of my favorite heroes was Dr. Robert Koch who beat Anthrax in Europe.

He did not merely beat Anthrax. To quote Wikipedia, Koch, "**As the founder of modern bacteriology,** identified the specific causative agents of tuberculosis, cholera, and anthrax and gave experimental support for the concept of infectious disease,[5] which included experiments on humans." At the time he began researching the method of how cows died from Anthrax in Europe. About half of all cows would die each year.  He identified the Anthrax bug via painstaking use of the experimental method, doing disgusting and dangerous work with diseased tissues and in the end proved how a certain microscopic, vile bacillus was the cause. He developed methods of finding and killing this bacillus and after Europeans began to use his methods, the  death of cows dropped almost 100%.  For this and other advances he won the Nobel Prize in 1905.

Because of my voracious reading habit I bumped into this great hero about age ten. Somehow, he became the great unsung hero no one knew about.. Biologists might know about him. But the average adult? Ask them who Dr. Robert Koch was and did; you will get Zip.

What factors were involved to turn me toward the written, spoken or sung word? Why did I enjoy opera and classical music so early in life? Was it a specific mentor? A significant concert or event? I have pondered these questions even from an early age. Why, for example, was I different from most of my peers in these areas? I heard popular music all my growing years. I watched and heard the birth of Rock & Roll with "Elvin" Presley, as my mother called him. 50 years later I remember most of the pop tunes of the day. But I yearned for a full symphony orchestra and found ways to attend symphonic concerts whenever possible. Why did I have a hugely, happy reaction to the news one day in about fifth grade at St. Barnabas when the teacher announced that we would be having a visit from a local symphony orchestra that morning and we would be allowed to see it? Why did most of the other kids mutter a protest under their breaths? "Do we have to?"

I don't believe there was any single person who led me to this path nor was there any significant, single event. I can't remember *not* loving the sound an orchestra makes. It was simply thrilling from my earliest memory and *still is*! I remember standing by a jukebox which St. Barnabas acquired when I was about 12. It was in the school basement where we used to play when the weather was bad. It contained about 40 songs. Most of them were pop songs of the day. But one was *Greensleeves*, played by a full symphony orchestra. It was the only symphonic piece on the jukebox. I played it over and over for the next few weeks, the sounds rushing over me. I remember standing there quietly listening with all my attention, letting the music sweep me into a higher elevation. Exactly the same effect hit me 20 years later when I heard the opening march of John Willliams' music *Star Wars*.

I have often thought if I have a religion, it does not involve a traditional god or creator of heaven and earth. My highest value is music. My Church of Music has two gods, Verdi and Mozart. My pope is Arturo Toscanini and my cardinals are people like my friend Maestro Stephen D. Wonder, Jimmy Levine, formerly of the Met, Seiji Ozawa, Georg Solti, Leonard Bernstein, Gustavo Dudamel. My bishops are the great singers who have made my life so much better; Ezio Pinza, Roberta Peters, Robert Merrill, Sherrill Milnes, Beverly Sills, Placido Domingo, Luciano Pavarotti, and "The Other Guy," Jose Carreras, Justino Díaz and Marilyn Horne. To hear any of theses artists is always a major, spiritual event.

Thus end my six years of daily absorption of Catholic mysticism. I was to go to a secular, local high school, Lakeside, where the Catholics were merely one group among many. About half of my peers from St. Barnabas went to a nearby Catholic high school. But the other half went to the secular school with me. My account of all this will continue as my parents, now aware of my intellectual rebellion, attempted

100

to have one more effort at bringing me back into the Catholic flock. It failed and I'll tell you why.

# Chapter 7 High School Freshman Year

I never graduated from St. Barnabas. In mid May of eighth grade my P's decided that the entire Archer Gang would drive to Bruno's graduation and commissioning ceremony at his midwest college and I would forego my ceremony. I guess they never thought I would want to stay and sing a special concert with my friends at St. Barnabas. We had got together a formidable quartet. I think it consisted of Moi, Boy, Malbun and Billy but I could be wrong. The point is, not only did I miss my graduation ceremony but also our graduation concert which was to be my last major musical effort there.

To this day I possess a color picture of Bruno standing on his collage quad on the day he received his commission as a Second Lieutenant in the Army in early June, 1959. He wore a ceremonial sword at his side and was very handsome. I stood behind him in the background smirking. I missed all my action back home because of the P's decision to take us all to his graduation instead of mine. Why couldn't we have done both?

I did not have time to reflect upon it because events were happening too fast. As soon as we returned home from Bruno's graduation I went to summer school for an English class at Lakeside High School. That was one large place! It had over 4,000 students when I went there. I first thing I noticed was that there was a huge difference in the development between freshman and seniors. Many freshman were short, skinny little boys compared to some of the seniors who were tall, relatively filled out and who actually needed to shave. They were grown men to me then. Freshman girls were little, skinny kids with no breasts as opposed to the senior women who were fully developed. For the next four years I enjoyed this atmosphere. It was, to quote, Tom Cruise as Maverick in *Top Gun*, ".....a target-rich environment."

Wanting to excel at singing and one day stand on the Met stage in New York, I thought I needed more theatrical experience. I found out that a play was about to start up (*Robin Hood*) which would be held on the Village Green in about a month. I went to the home of the producer who, by chance, lived less than two blocks from me. I told him of my desire to get more stage experience and he told me to see the director and he would arrange a meeting for me. Auditions had already been held but the announcement of who would play what role had not been released. Disappointed, I told the producer that I was not choosy and would do any role I was given.

Ah Ye of Little Faith! In the next day or two I met the director who turned out to be a very voluptuous woman of about 40. She looked me over and said, "Do you think you could play the part of Robin?" I was stunned. She was offering me the lead within ten minutes of meeting her? I told her that I had portrayed a priest, so I guess I could play an archer who lived in a forest. As it turned out, the play was performed with the actors merely walking around the outdoor stage area to a taped narration with music. I would neither sing nor speak in this role. I think now that in performances at this juvenile stage, the director was hurting for a tall boy willing to play the part since boys are reluctant to sing or dance at age 13.

We did the play with me as the star/non star. The girl who played Maid Marion was very good looking and I fell for her immediately. I even took her on a "date" which consisted of walking from the Village Green to a sweet-shop with her one day after a performance. It never turned into anything significant because I met another girl at about the same time. The whole theatrical effort was rather simple and did not seem to teach me much. Real, learning, acting experience would take place about five months later on the stage at my new high school.

Meanwhile I was cutting lawns, going to the beach at Lake Michigan, removing the green, grass clippings from the cuffs of my pants and socializing with our gang at the beach. The gang had grown and increased in variety. It now consisted of a base of St. Barnabas boys from my class, and a bevy of girls who graduated from Lincoln Middle School and were about to attend high school for the first time. This new group included Catholics, protestants and Jews. From our male perspective, we really did not care what their religion was, we went for looks and how well they treated us.

It was in this splendid milieu that I met a girl my age who was just out of Lincoln Middle and headed for Lakeside. Her name was Laura Polenzani and she had smooth, clear, tan skin, and lived toward the center of town and had a pool at her home. That summer she invited us (Us was usually my little gang, Me, Boy, Bar, Malbun, Billy) to swim at her pool on a daily basis which we did many, many times that summer. If you have concluded by now that I liked her for her pool you would be dead wrong. Malbun had moved to a new home that had a pool so I did not need a girlfriend with a pool. I was attracted to her because she was good looking and attentive to me.

It was in this swirl of new acquaintances that we began a tradition which lasted all through high school...the make out party. That summer of 1959, when I was three months away from my 14th birthday, I discovered a wondrous thing. One night we were at Linda Goldblatt's pad near the beach. Fifties music was coming from a stack of 45's on the stereo. It was a typical make out party mostly taking place in Linda's large basement.

I was there with Laura and we were slow dancing and kissing. Then things began to get slightly hotter when the lights were turned very low. I found a little door to the laundry room and as soon as Laura and I got in there she seemed to know exactly *why* we went in because our kissing became much more passionate, our tongues getting in overtime. Jay Leno was once asked if he had erections when he grew up. His answer? "Of course, wasn't that pretty much all through high school?" I found that remark of his intensely funny because it was so true. A perfect example was that night with Laura. Our bodies pressed together, my genitalia beginning to press against her. To be more precise, my pants pressing against her skirt.

106

my body firm against her. Our breaths were coming faster and louder. It was in this position, standing in the dark in that laundry room that we began to undulate together, faster and faster until we released our needs. What a euphemism! I released *my* need. I don't know for sure if she did. I discovered that girls like sex too! I was overjoyed. All my future life I would try to make them happy. I had discovered the joys of what we then called, "dry-humping."

We did not discuss what we had just done. But we did it for the next year or so every time we had a chance. We knew that it was safe and could not result in pregnancy. It was far from actual intercourse, but a safe step. I wanted to go all the way but I had heard so many stories of how enjoying ten minutes of bliss could lead to having to quit school, get married to support a wife and baby. It was not even coitus interruptus which I knew was no real protection. It was a temporary fix but it had some psychological benefits. I was very happy to share these intense physical and intimate moments with her. She reciprocated in that she trusted me to please her but not hurt her.

Once again six years of Catholic brainwashing was comfortably forgotten. Dry-humping was probably a sin against the All High, a duet of self abuse, and spilling of seed. Yet it actually hurt no one and gave us sexual release. Only the mystics could find a way to make a simple physical act between two consenting people into a major offense.

My parents tried one more time to get me back in the religious fold. They commanded me to go to high school religious instruction at St. Barnabas one evening a week. I did not fight this. Because I knew that Laura had been dragooned into this nonsense too. So instead of becoming good Catholics again we spent the time making out in the library.

I played football on the freshman team in September. High school football employed the basics which I had learned in grammar school but everything moved faster and the players were more dedicated and stronger. I remember early on in scrimmage I tackled one of the running backs who became our varsity fullback three years later. I nailed him very low, too low in one respect but he went down quickly to my satisfaction. When I stood up I felt a foreign object in my mouth. What the heck was that? It turned out I struck the guy's foot with my teeth and chipped the corner of one of my incisors. I looked at the chip and threw it away. To this day that incisor has a gentle curve of missing surface. At the time I tackled him it was very sharp but over the years it's worn down.

I loved the game. I felt no compunction at throwing my entire body at an opponent in a giant, full-body block. In a sophomore/freshman scrimmage, I distinctly remember attempting to tackle a sophomore back who was very fast and very strong. It was like tackling a moving steel robot. I grabbed him but he burst through me and I lost him. But one time I happened to overhear the opponents in their huddle give away the next play. Knowing who was going to get the ball and which way he was supposed to run, I blitzed the defense and mowed the runner down with a perfect tackle for which I was complimented by the coach. I made the mistake of telling the coach that I had overheard the play which had allowed me to confidently blitz. He told me I should not have admitted this because it denigrated his version of what I had just done.

Football was my main interest the first few month at Lakeside. Music was a strong second and girls were all over the place and I could not get enough of all those attractions. On the practice field I mostly enjoyed what we were doing. The only thing I hated were wind sprints. We were lined up on the field at one end. The coach would blow his whistle and we would be instructed to run straight down to-ward the other end of the field as hard as we could. After we ran 20 or 30 yards down the field the whistle would blow. We would stop and line up again. The whistle would blow and we would again take off as fast as we could. It was exhausting and terribly hard. It was designed to toughen us up and maybe catch an opponent who had somehow got through our defense, broken free and might be running for a touchdown against us. Wind sprints were designed to make us tough enough and strong enough to run after an opponent and catch him before he got to our goal. I understood its purpose but that did not make it any easier.

Again I noticed a wide range of physical characteristics between different guys. One of the assistant coaches was a large, ruddy-faced man about 40 years in age. His face was reddish and as smooth as a pingpong ball. Once he and one of my teammates were standing close together. My teammate must have been 14 years old like me but he had a slightly darker complexion and his whiskers looked like he was thirty. My peer's whiskers made the assistant coach's face look like a little boy's. That was one of the many surprises I observed those first few months in high school. But I learned something from it. You can't get a really fair idea of someone from their mere appearance. How many whiskers one has ends up being irrelevant. My peer with the dark, whiskery face turned out to be only an average football player. One of the toughest, best players on my team had a baby face.

My freshman team played all of our league's games the same as the varsity and we compiled a good record. One of the highlights of those games was when we played a game up north where the opposition had a Gargantuan fullback. I was playing left end on defense and one of my long time friends from St. Barnabas, who had also gone to Lakeside with me, was playing left outside linebacker. On one play the giant fullback swept around his end directly toward me. I attacked him and attempted to tackle him. But he was so big and fast that I merely bumped into him, only slowing him down a bit. But after that, Murr, my St Barnabas peer, came up and dispatched the immense fullback to the ground. I felt embarrassed that I could not get the guy down. Murr told me I had done fine, getting the monster slowed down and ready for the tackle.

Bruno was a brother of amazing characteristics. He was tall, musical, scholarly and invented things! Or should I say *attempted* to invent things. He had Chief's help too with his inventions. The first one was supposed to be an underwater breath-

111

ing device which Bruno built out of wood and rubber tubing. As I remember it was nothing more than a hollow, thin, wood box with an opening for air on the top and another, smaller opening on the bottom which was the port for the air hose connection. The idea was for the aquanaut, Bruno, to place the breathing hose inside his mouth and dive underwater breathing through this tube (I think they used a standard, 1/2 inch garden hose.) while the box floated on the surface. It was tried once and abandoned. The Great Aquanaut could not get enough air into his lungs because he had to suck it all the way through a long tube without any pressure (Which a proper aqua-lung provides.)

While I was at St. Barnabas fifth through eighth grade, Bruno was at a prestigious, Catholic University. He started a tradition which I followed while I was the Army, years later. He wrote a marvelous letter each week, typed, single spaced, very few errors, multi-page no less, to our family back home. He called these letters "Epistles" in the manner of St. Paul. He started freshman year with Epistle #1 and ended up four years later sending communiques numbered in triple digits. These missives covered many of the things he was studying, his grades, usually no lower than 90 out of 100 and other topics such as his activities in the university symphony, his suite mates, his hilarious descriptions of All-American football players who lived

group that performed these shows was the "Opera Group" which one had to be a junior or senior to belong.

While singing in the freshman group for boys, I did not wait to get on the stage. The students at Lakeside also put on a student-written, student- -directed and student-performed show each winter called *Prodigy Largess*. I tried out for this one afternoon singing "Once in Love With Amy." I waited about a week for the announcement to be posted on the music department bulletin board as to was selected to play in the show. I looked down the list of names for mine. There it was, Ben Archer. I got in on my first try. I was a little let down by hearing that, as usual, the directors were hurting for boys to get into the show and would have taken any male with a beating heart.

It was rehearsing on the Lakeside stage in the next few months that I heard some advice that I never forgot. We all knew about singing coaches, directors and other people who made shows work. But this time we, the entire cast, was assembled to hear words of advice from the TD. TD? Touchdown? No, in this case TD was short for Technical Director. The technical director is responsible for all the props, stage sets, lighting and virtually all the objects that go into a show. As such he's higher than almost everyone but the director himself.

He was a senior and spoke to us very seriously. His speech was something like this,

*"You are the singers and actors in this show. You may think you are the stars but you can't be a star without a small army of people running the lights, the sets and props. Remember this above all else, we can make you shine but we can make you look horrible too. So come on this stage and act professionally. Know your lines, listen to your director and the techies who will bring that light up or down as needed and above all don't play with curtains, sets, ropes or any props. We run them. You sing or act. We run the rest. Do not attempt to tell us our jobs. We will not tell you how to sing. If you fail to remember these rules you may find a green light focused on your forehead which will make you look stupid and silly."*

One very naive freshman girl who had been picked for her ample figure, later asked, "If I get the green light on my forehead, how do I get it off? Will soap remove it?" The words of this TD suited me fine. I had already come to pretty much the same conclusion based on the needs of the show itself. How could it function if the cast was always goofing off and playing around with the props?

Another facet of the music department at Lakeside was that we were frequently given individual instruction in music by noted professionals. During my time in school, one of the greatest voice coaches, who later sang at the Met as its leading baritone, Sherrill Milnes, walked the halls of our school. I remember the first time I heard him sing in one of our larger music rooms. Before he sang he addressed us with some advice about singing generally and then announced his song. His speaking voice itself was like a gigantic, bass drum, echoing off the walls and penetrating our ears. The song he chose was a light number from a show of the era. Here's a shot of Milnes playing Scarpia:

*Photo: Louis Melancon, @Metropolitan Opera*

118

The mastermind and leading figure in the Music Department was the head of the whole department, Dr. Jack Abrams. My parents raved about him and how well he had treated Aubere several years earlier. From the very start I could see why everyone adored him. He was a short man but full of confidence. When he raised his hands to start a song he had everyone's eyes upon him. His comments were famous for their brevity and intelligence. He led the senior Boy's Ensemble, chose and directed the opera each year. For the next four years I nicknamed him Dr. Jack. We all genuinely thought he was one step higher than god. and we liked him. Eventually, we became great friends and he later coached me personally in voice.

When some of my freshman peers found out I was going to sing in the student production *Prodigy Largess*, they began to make fun of me, implying that singing on stage was for "fruits." Fruits was a word in the 50's which meant one was less than manly. And what was this obsession I had with stupid orchestral music? That was "soooo dumb" these critics maintained. I made a bet with one of them. I maintained that before we graduated one of them would fall pretty hard for a girl and if she was a singer, dancer or orchestra performer then, after observing more closely what she did, their views would change exactly 180 degrees. This prediction was met with guffaws and snickers.

In senior year one of the same nay-sayers began to go with an orchestra player who had done all the shows and concerts during our years at school together. He came up to me sheepishly one afternoon senior year and recalled his attitude about the performing arts in freshman year and admitted it was completely based on ignorance and that my prediction was correct. I told him I was disappointed that we had not put money on it. Oddly, the exact same kind of thing happened to me in Alaska in the 80's. One of my friends, a macho Alaskan guy, used to make fun of the fact that my Main Squeeze and I were always going to symphonies (Which he called sim pa thies) and operas. He could not imagine a real man doing such a thing. I made the same prediction to him. Less than a year later he was introduced to a girl who played in the Anchorage Symphony and before you know it he was attending her rehearsals and concerts. It was not very long before he too came to me with the same sheepish attitude and admitted he was living in a whole new and better world and actually looked forward to the music she played.

120

Freshman year I was re-introduced to Homer's *Odyssey* in English class and I really enjoyed it. My father and Bruno's performances had made me very ready to take it on for myself. I remember one day in class I was expressing to the teacher and my classmates my amazement at how superstitious the sailers were by being unduly influenced by large birds flying over their ships as great omens of good or bad fortunes. I did not at the time remember what kind of birds Homer had mentioned so I complained about all the buzzard omens in the tale. The class and the teacher broke out into a loud chorus of laughter. I guess it made a major difference that the birds were not buzzards but eagles.

I developed many friends, associates and strange peers during my four years at Lakeside. One of them was John Beard. He was the son of a doctor and one young man who, in today's lingo, "thought outside of the box." In freshman year he attempted to trip me as I entered a classroom. I stumbled but did not fall. John was not a big guy and as I came up to him he looked terrified that I was going to seek major revenge. Instead I serenely told him to attempt to trip me any time he could and I would never fall. I gave him carte blanche to trip me for the next four years.

He did every so often but by the end of senior year he never got me down. Why? Because I was such a graceful Fred Astaire type? No. Because I walked ever so carefully always watching out for potential minefields set by peers? Definitely not. It was because I had what I termed, "A good understanding." That was really just saying I had big feet.

John called me up one day and told me he had acquired a case of Mogen David Wine and had no place to store it. Did I have a place? I told him I could stash it underneath my neighbor's doghouse which I had easy access to by merely stepping around a huge, old tree. Later that day John came over lugging a large case of Mogen David wine in bottles. We stuck it under the dog house. I told him he could come and get it or parts of it anytime he wanted, just not to let my parents see him. I knew or at least, had major suspicions, as to how he had acquired it. He lifted it from a synagogue not far from where he lived. I told him I did not want to know the details and he nodded in agreement. He told me to try one of the bottles. Having tried some of the wine at St. Barnabas years earlier and finding it terrible, I was reluctant to try any of his purloined booty. But one day my curiosity got the better of me. I went to the stash and opened one of the bottles. It was, if anything, as bad, or worse, than the Catholic wine. John eventually came and removed the rest of the

Mogen David from under the doghouse. I don't think I ever asked him what he did with it. It was so vile I did not care..


To conclude my account of my freshman year in high school I want to reminisce on the park in the north end of my town near St. Barnabas. As I wrote earlier, it was an important place of much of my youth, playing softball, football and ice skating in the winter months when it was flooded by city workers. When it was below 32 degrees F, the park made an excellent skating rink. It was large, flat and had only one obstacle in it, a large tree directly in the middle. It was there that I learned how to skate, gradually becoming more and more confident and fast. We played all sorts of games on that ice. As we got a bit older we would dance with girls, gliding, twirling duets to waltz music which came over the PA system. As the winters progressed and more snow fell on the ice, city workers would use light pickup trucks to push most of the snow toward one end. It gradually built up into a large mound of the white stuff...perfect for racing as fast as we could and then leaping into it in a blaze of snowy happiness. As teenagers we used to try to get girls to join us on those mounds for icy make out sessions.

One evening my gang, (Me, Boy, Bar, Billy) was ice skating at this wintry park and I felt a bit mischievous. Inside the warming shelter I asked the attendant if I could make a short announcement. He looked at me and paused, as if he were debating how sincere I was. After a short pause he let me do it, handing me the mike. He turned off the music playing on the two loudspeakers. I paused and then began in a serious but trembling voice. "I just wanted to thank you all for all your well wishes after the death of my grandmother who passed recently at the age of 87. All the priests and people of St. Barnabas were most kind. The funeral mass was well attended" I noticed that the attendant looked as if he were about to cry. Then I said, softly and quietly, "At least the baby lived.

# Chapter 8 Sophomore year, Philosophy, Youth

After Bruno graduated from his university he planned to get married to a very attractive Mexican Babe named LM. The only problem with this was that she lived in Mexico City. So, after much soul-searching my old man decided to take all the rest of the Archer Gang to Mexico to see this marriage ceremony .

The night before we moved out on this international adventure Chief displayed in his hands what I only could think of as a fortune. Where did he get all this dough? In 1959 gas averaged 25 cents a gallon. One could buy a decent home for $12,400. He showed us the money he had removed from his savings, a full twelve hundred bucks in the form of twelve, hundred dollar bills. At this moment I knew we were not poor; we had never been poor; we were middle class people. That Gargantuan sum was to pay for our entire family, sans Bruno, who flew down to Mexico, to eat, travel and board from Chicago to Mexico and back. There would be six in all, Chief, Zombie, Aubere, Woban, Pendron and I riding in an old Mercury station wagon.

Off we motored in early June of 1960, the six of us talking., laughing, singing. As we left the Chicago area we began to see things I had never seen, Gigantic trucks, colorful Burma Shave signs arrayed in rows along the highway, Howard Johnsons.

As we traveled south and slightly west, our tempers grew thin and battles broke out as to where we should eat, where we should stop and sleep for the night. I was slightly amazed as a 14 year old because I was still a boy in many ways. Since Chief was paying for the whole trip, ought not *he* make all these decisions? And Pendron, age 16, my brother closest in age to me, was a particular participant in these battles. He got into more than one fist fight with Chief or Aubere before the whole trip finished.

For the first time I saw reddish earth! What in the world? Earth, dirt, ground, soil, terra firma; to me it had always been Midwestern, black, rich, Illinois loam. In Oklahoma the ground was a very real, reddish/orangish color.

We warped through Illinois, Missouri, Oklahoma, Texas and finally down at Loredo, Texas we encountered the border of Mexico. My old man was ready for this. The president of Mexico, an average crook named Adolfo Lopez Mateos, happened to have visited Chicago that year and my father had arranged for a friend to take a clear, B&W picture of Chief and him together. I remember this picture with great clarity. It was a large, 8 X 10 glossy and Chief kept it in a tough container to keep it unwrinkled and in good shape. On more than one occasion, other than the border guards, Chief would take the large picture out and show it around. We did not have much trouble from Mexican bureaucrats.

M y

pop is

stand-

ing on the left with glasses and bow tie, hand extended shaking with the then president of
Mexico. Note the security guy on the extreme left watching my dad's hand to see if he had a
gun or knife!

After Nuevo Laredo we pushed into Mexican deserts, little towns and big cities. We drove through Monterrey and San Luis Potosi before we finally arrived in Mexico City, DF. At one point the engine began to steam up so we had to find a mechanic to fix it. The B&W of Chief and the Mexican President came out on that occasion. I don't remember how many long days, (They seemed much more hot and torturous because our old station wagon had no air conditioning!) it took us to finally get to Mexico City but even when there, Chief refused to ask for help to find the hotel we had been booked in by Bruno. We wound around and around for over three hours, before Chief finally called Bruno who was already there to advise us on how to get from one part of this giant city to our hotel.

By the way, before we left our home in Illinois I noticed a short tube laying under our rear bumper. I don't know what it was for but my Red Ryder BB gun fit inside it perfectly in such a way that you could not see the stock even if you were looking. I was able to take it out at night and plink away at cans and such when we were parked at various motels. I was terrified that the border guards would find it and confiscate it. But they missed it and I was able to shoot my BB gun in all the places we stopped with the exception of Mexico DF; it was too crowded to be able to shoot without people knowing about it.

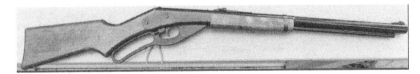

We had all been told that we must not drink water from a tap, eat salads or other foods which dripped in local water. If we did we could get *"Trots,"* the *"Mexican Two Step,"* a form of mild to even serious diarrhea. I think most of us *did* get it. Can you imagine you are getting married in a large, cathedral to a very beautiful Mexican lady with many dignitaries and high Catholic officials about. Now imagine taking part in this long, Catholic ceremony with a good case of diarrhea? Bruno got it the night before he was to be married. His story later was that he prayed to God to relieve him of this pain at least for the ceremony and the official parts thereafter. And, according to Bruno, God heard him and granted his wish. I got a short case of it and had to hang about the bathroom for several days.

We noticed that Mexico City DF had many Roundabouts, what Mexicans call "Glorietas." Some of these Glorietas connected not just two streets but on many, three or more streets. There would be a large ring of streets with little walkways for pedestrians between them. We found that we would go up to the Glorieta, wait until there was no traffic on the first street, run across to the in-between part and wait, run across to the next part and so on. This took some time as the traffic was fast and seemed to never stop. One time as we were crossing one of these Glorietas, Aubere remarked, "What would a blind man do? How

130

would he know when there was no traffic?" Bruno responded without a pause in a decisive voice, "There *are no* blind men here."

Bruno was the only one of us including Chief who had even the smallest ability to speak Spanish. My father, when speaking to Mexicans would speak louder or add an "o" to certain words thinking it would translate to Spanish but it never did. Once when we were in the hotel restaurant Chief asked Bruno to order milk for Pendron and me, the two youngest kids. So Bruno spoke to the waiter in his sophisticated version of Spanish and, ten minutes later out came Pendron and my drinks...except they were beers.

The marriage took place in a gigantic cathedral. Instead of priests conducting the marriage mass, there were a string of bishops and cardinals. From my point of view, I thought I saw the Pope once but he was covered up by all the glitter, pomp and circumstance. LM was from a very Catholic and influential family indeed. At the high point of a Catholic Mass, the Transubstantiation, it is traditional to have an altar boy ring a little bell three times which sounds like..."tink, tink, tink." But a little bell at this majestic ceremony? No way. They had three, very ornamented trumpets playing a harmonic, three note blast!

131

It's interesting that I remember these events from that over-two-week adventure. I don't remember the ride home at all. We had the same six people in the old station wagon. We had the same 2,096 miles to cover. I remember being very happy to get home at last.

Sophomore year I tried out for and was accepted again, into our student production *Prodigy Largess*. I was to be in shows, sing solos and generally do music a lot all four years at Lakeside. Looking back at it, I really enjoyed most aspects of putting on musicals, learning the songs, the first stage rehearsals, the first tech rehearsals with full orchestra, the whole bit. But I had a weakness, my ability to learn and remember musical lines was highly limited. The fear, of being on stage with a spot-light on me, about to belt out a number... forgetting the opening lines! That is one reason I never got into straight drama. At least with music you have the additional help of the music itself.

Until I was 14 years old I thought we were the poorest family in my town. Why? For many reasons. To put it in context, we lived in a small oasis of wealth and privilege. Many of the homes on the north side of town were mansions. The town had one of the highest, average incomes in the world and many of the men who lived here were CEO's, captains of industry, or high-level government bureaucrats. Most, but not all, of my friend's fathers were very successful men with big to humongous homes. Relative to my peers I was on the poor side.

Yet we had a fairly large home with five bedrooms, two full baths, a basement and large porches on each end of our home. But! Until about 1961, we had no rugs, no private car, no TV, no vacations to nice places in the winter, no weekly allowance. I wore mostly hand-me-downs that my brothers had worn almost threadbare. In fact Bruno, who was eight years older than me, was pictured in his school album at Lakeside wearing an old, plaid shirt, in June of 1951. Eight years later I wore the exact same shirt my freshman year!!! I can remember Zombie's refrain, "If you waste food (or whatever) we will be at the County Poor House in no time flat."

It was not until my sophomore year, when I became taller than my brothers that I suddenly noticed we had money to buy me actual new, store-bought shirts and pants! I can still hear my father's voice in the winter, "Ben! Close the door! I'm not rich enough to heat the world!" After Bruno and Aubere left the nest, I guess we had more money to spend on things like rugs, a TV and a private car. Until then my father drove a company car which we were not supposed to ride in. Oddly, it had a built-in telephone which I learned how to use. My father, being an engineer, had some *side* benefits.

I loved grand opera, movie musicals and even legitimate drama and Broadway shows. I loved almost any formal use of the spoken word. At that time my favorite actor was the Englishman, James Mason. Mason played many very different roles in his long career. He was especially good at playing upper-class English types. When he spoke his words were definitive, intelligent, suave and honest. His acting and delivery were such that one immediately believed him and liked him. Fifteen-year-old Ben Archer, now six feet tall with a deep voice began to inhale all this. Deeply.

The first few days of classes I found out about a new girl in our class. She was a knockout. I had heard about her and how fine she was from head to toe. Several days later I finally set my eyes upon her. She was even better than the rumors I had heard. She was just straight knock down sexy with a great figure on the slim side, bright face and jet-black hair, the equal of any Hollywood starlet. I did not actually meet her for several weeks. During that time, my imagination ran wild. Not only would she accompany me on dates, but she would be able to sing duets with me. We would knock over our school's student-led shows with an act that would make Fred Astaire and Ginger Rogers look like an amateur hour. Plus, she would be the best make-out queen of all teenagers in the world.

The day came when I finally met her. Up close, she was even more beautiful than I had observed from 20 feet. When introduced to me she asked me how I was and how tall I

134

was. Her voice was a true *Abomination unto the Lord*! It was a hideous combination of screeching, neighing like a horse and fingernails on a chalkboard. All my dreams sank into the depths of despair! This babe was a visual delight but an audio disaster. I don't even remember her name. I politely answered her questions but managed to quickly disengage.

There comes into all of our lives, times that are not pleasant, or even disgusting and not usually spoken about. But they are part of life and ought to be added into the whole in order to make the picture of reality, well, *real*. This next memory is one of those incidents that is in the unpleasant, close to disgusting part of life.

One day when I was about 16 or so, I was in my room goofing off when my father walked in. He was bare chested which was unusual for him, even in our home. He got right to the point. "Hey Ben, " he said, "I've got a problem on my back and I can't reach it. Can you take a look?" Curious, I looked at his back which was very white because his great, year around tan was arms and head only, as in a golfer's tan. He crooked an arm around and with his thumb showed me where the spot was. I saw it immediately. It was a large, rather ugly blackhead, maybe a 1/16th of an inch in diameter, or bigger. As a teenager I knew what he wanted me to do. I told him what I saw, hoping he would have some professional deal with it but he said, "Can you squeeze it?"

135

So I was condemned to see this thing through. I washed my hands which pleased him very much but he did not tell me so. I then asked him to move toward the window so I could see the area better. He complied. Then I placed my thumbs on both sides of this monster and began to apply pressure. It didn't take much because right away a bluish, off-whitish emission began to extrude, with the consistency of an old hunk of toothpaste. It was amazing and it kept coming. After a few seconds a perfect tube of this stuff emitted, about an inch and a half, with no end in sight. I switched my thumbs from pressing on the sides to pressing from the top and bottom. The odious discharge kept coming as I pressed, starting to curve around into a perfect curlicue. It was about five inches long when my thumbs tired. I told him what was happening as I pressed and he laughed and said, "Keep Going!" I went into the bathroom and took some toilet paper and gently removed the curlicue and showed him. He took the paper and went into the bathroom and flushed it down the toilet. Then he said, "Is there more?"

There was more...a lot more. I continued the pressure, changing direction every minute or so until I had removed maybe a full seven inches all together. I then took more tissue and cleansed the area with rubbing alcohol. The entire repugnant matter was finished. Chief was satisfied. I felt a little like Androcles and the Lion. My real problem is that I remember it is so clearly and would rather not.

136

Sophomore year I went to my first opera at a world-class opera house, The Chicago Lyric Opera. The opera was *Prince Igor* by Alexander Borodin, starring the great Bulgarian bass, Boris Christoff. I was stunned at the sheer power and beauty of the soloists and chorus. I was already a confirmed opera buff but seeing this opera helped turn me into a life-long opera fanatic. Then something most strange and mercurial happened. Out of the wings flew a human being who seemed to be doing barrel rolls and walking on air. He was the recent Russian defector, ballet star Rudolf Nureyev. He was the most amazing dancer I'd ever seen, his every move so graceful, so powerful, so dramatic, that I could not take my eyes off him. The audience, as one, was taken the same way. He completely upstaged Christoff. My very first, live opera and I saw two of the greatest performers ever in their respective fields.

I found the listing of *Prince Igor* in the Chicago Lyric Opera archives online. I removed many of the cast names but left three in:

## The Chicago Lyric Opera

## *Prince Igor*

## by Alexander Borodin

## Cast:

| Prince Igor: | Igor Goon |
|---|---|
| Kohchak: | Boris Christoff |
| Solo Dancer: | Rudolf Nureyev |

There was a bonus. I saw *three* of the greatest performers in the world. Before the opera even started I noticed a future superstar standing in the lobby waiting patiently to take his seat. He was future Metropolitan Opera baritone Sherrill Milnes, who was kind enough to actually recognize us from our presence at Lakeside musical functions. Milnes, who was not yet a star at the Met, taught voice at Lakeside. He greeted us with a voice which was a gigantic, deep, tympanic drum, echoing and mellifluous at the same time. He asked us our names and if we wanted to sing opera at Lakeside and beyond. I told him I had wanted to do this since I was about four. He laughed at that response. He was about 6'4" and all bets indicated he would be a big star when he reached the Met. Several years later he arrived at the Met and for the next twenty seasons, he was the leading baritone in the world! For visual and auditory proof of my last statement, go to your computer, go to this link, turn your volume up and sit back for perfection!

<https://www.youtube.com/watch?v=5eZLPU3mpBQ>

Football season I watched from the sidelines as my teammates from freshman year, now bigger, taller and stronger, played every Saturday against the entire range of our league's opponents. I was sidelined by order of the head of the Lakeside Athletic Department. It seems several weeks after football season my freshman year, someone, I never found out who, had seen me smoking a cigarette several blocks from Lakeside outside a little store. I was ordered to return the letter I had earned and kicked off the team until Junior year. It was all cut and dried. No appeal, no discovery, no chance to defend myself. Maybe this was because I admitted smoking near the school. I had broken no school rules so the school itself was not after me. Apparently, the Athletic Department had its own interpretation of smoking and where it could and could not be done. Perhaps I should have lied and denied smoking and demanded to see and confront whoever had accused me. But I thought the whole thing bogus and walked out. Sophomore year I returned to wrestling.

I wrestled all four years at Lakeside in the intramural program. I had to weigh in at the start of the program. All four years I wrestled at 165 pounds. Freshman year I weighed a bit less, sophomore year almost exactly 165, junior and senior years I had to lose a few pounds to weigh a maximum of 168 to wrestle at 165. Each class would engage in as many bouts as there were competitors. In other words, if 50 freshman boys signed up for the wrestling competition, there would be 25 first round bouts. The winners of the first round would wrestle the winners in the second round, each time cutting the remaining wrestlers

139

numbers in half until one was the class winner. All four classes did this. They wrestled their own classmates until there were four, class winners. Then the freshman winner would wrestle the junior winner and the sophomore winner would take on the senior. In my case, I won my class bouts each year after three or four matches. Freshman year I wrestled the junior and lost to him on points. Sophomore year I won my class section and lost to the senior on points. Junior and senior years I won all my class bouts and beat the underclassmen. All four years I had about 24 matches, won 22 of them and was never pinned.

I enjoyed wrestling because it was fast, required some muscle and planning and one could see up front who was competent and who was not. One day I wrestled a guy who sweated so badly he was like the proverbial "greased pig." I was getting the better of him and hoped to pin the guy but he would literally squeeze out of my holds by wiggling! At one point I took a towel into the ring and began to dry him off. I was stopped by the ref but he saw what was happening and ordered the guy to towel himself off which he reluctantly did. Then when the match resumed I was quickly able to win. For winning these matches each year I was given a commemoration made of felt indicating my victories in wrestling. I still have them to this day, half a century years later.

By sophomore year my interests were not merely sports and music. My reading had forced me to continue examining the issue of the existence of God. I bumped into Bertrand

140

Russell's *Why I Am Not a Christian.* I read every word of that essay about three times. I was impressed with this no end because Russell writes so beautifully and clearly. On many of the issues he brought up, I had already come to the same conclusions on my own. My analysis was gradually becoming more thorough and methodical.

Russell considered the mystics' argument: "Nothing springs up by itself. Everything needs a creator. The Earth and all of existence had to have a creator. That creator, therefore, is God." Russell answered this basic mystical thrust the same way I did. By that logic, God would need to be created too. Who created Him? Thus the famous, endless regress that gets you nowhere. I reasoned even before I read Russell that if anything "always was and always would be" it is reality itself. I came to this conclusion because I had read about the law in physics called "Conservation of Matter and Energy." It states that matter and energy don't go away, they merely change form and weigh the same. When one is converted into the other they both continue to exist. There is no reason to insert a God as the creator.

As time went on I would gradually read every book I could find by Bertrand Russell. With the exception of his *Principia*, his giant tome on mathematics. (Even my brainy brother Bruno admitted that only seven people in the whole world understood that book, he, not being one of them.) I savored Russell's rational and kind position on most issues,

141

with the exception of his economics, which I felt were built on sand; he acquired them in 1898 in Berlin of all places.

In the Fall I met for the first time, two, flesh and blood atheists. I met them at a party one Saturday night. They were engaged in a calm but lively argument with a believer of some sort. The believer argued that without a God, men would become beasts and kill, rape and pillage instead of following the Ten Commandments. The atheists were agile debaters. One of them came back with, "Kill, rape and pillage huh? You mean like the Crusaders killed, raped and pillaged their way across Europe and into the Middle East? You mean how Roman Catholic Church authorities, with the explicit permission of the Pope, engaged in the slaughter of Jews, witches, unrepentant Christians, old women with money and others they disagreed with and saw some profit in dispatching to the Grand Inquisitor?" The atheists added that men could observe the world about them and note how men needed to follow an ethics of some kind. They were capable of forming their own ethics without a god ordering them to do so. Then there were the additional questions, Is a human act morally correct in and of itself or only because God commands it? How would anyone be able to know the difference?

I sat there listening and watching because while I agreed with the atheists, they seemed to have a much greater understanding of the whole debate than I did. I kept my

142

mouth shut but learned a lot from these fellows. Malbun for instance, never got beyond the First Cause Argument. We **debated** that very issue for the next 50 years but he held onto First Cause like a giant, very muscular Bulldog with a bone. He never took the time to read Russell or Rand or any of the other famous, atheist writers.

The subject of atheism broadened into a more basic, Mysticism against Reason debate. It could be summed up as: One argues on the basis of facts, logic and reason, having acquired the facts through "checkable" processes known as the "Scientific Method." Or, one could argue on the wisdom of an old book, authority, emotion and power from the top down. Interestingly, the authors of this old book, never knew what caused the seasons to follow each other, or that the earth revolved around the sun, or that disease is caused by particular microbes. The Biblical authors had never seen a microscope, never used calculus, never even saw a mechanical, spring-driven watch. They were, relative to modern writers, completely ignorant of science or the practical effects of cause and effect.

For the rest of my life I was to expand my understanding of this argument. I have never changed my mind about the total irrationality of mysticism. I wonder, to this day, how mystics can actually keep the terribly weak ideas they hold.

15-year-old Ben Archer was not all music and drama waiting to happen, although that year I began to sing in concerts before various crowds. I remember one night that first semester I sang "Old Man River" from *Show Boat* by Jerome Kern at a parents night gathering. I brought a single prop with me, a long hoe with a wooden handle. I had no problem with the number which is written for a bass voice. It was a number that I could knock out, and did regularly, for the next fifty years. But my acting left some people wondering. I probably did not deal with the prop very well. Oh well, live and learn. The problem was that while I was given superior vocal training, I received no dramatic training at all! This was to haunt me again seriously in senior year.

As I was writing, before I so rudely interrupted myself, I was not an all-good guy. If you remember in earlier chapters, I described how my friends and I went on D-Nights frequently. Usually, our main goal was to hop pools and chase girls or try to get into hen parties. But on one occasion and one occasion, and *only one*, Malbun and I, plus a few others, went on what I immediately termed, (while we were doing it) a solo "Destructo D-Night." This was in almost direct contradiction to all the other stuff we did growing up. We took our BB gun rifles with us and, as we walked along, we competed to see who could blast out the next street light, one after the other, leaving a trail of darkness behind us. The street lights in our town were naked bulbs with a circular, metal plate above them to protect them from rain. Your BB might strike the metal plate with a telling metallic sound. The "telling metallic sound" was, "You missed!" If you struck the naked bulb it would shatter, grow bright like a star going Nova and then turn dark.

As we walked along we blasted out the lights. If one wanted to, one could have followed us by the trail of blackened street lights. That night I thought to myself while we were destroying these lights, "This is wrong. I'll have to write about it some day and ask myself why we did it." That day is now and I still have no answer. We kept going and by the time our first and only "Destructo D-Night" finished, we had probably shattered over a hundred street lights. I think the problem is in our DNA. We humans can do the most generous, loving acts. An hour later we are wreaking havoc on street lights! And if one chalks it up to being an undeveloped teenager, that alone can't account for it because one can see adults of all ages avoiding moral thinking while committing crimes of various sorts.

I'm not proud of that night. I'm proud of the fact that we *never did it again*. We got away with it. But it did not make my life happier. I wonder what it cost the taxpayer to have city workers drive along our route replacing the blasted bulbs? I'm happy to report that I have never again in my short life engaged in this kind of thoughtless violence.

Sophomore year Boy and I discovered we could go to the movies at a nearby outdoor theater for half price. My date and I would climb into the cavernous trunk of "Betsy the Blue Bitch," Boy's old Buick, at a nearby, closed, gas station. Boy would then drive into the outdoor theater and lift the trunk door and we would emerge. Now and then we would watch the movies, in-between make out sessions. Boy would pay for himself and his date at the entrance and I would pay half of that.

This all worked well, except I would also have to convince a girl to climb into the trunk with me. "It's only for five minutes while Boy drives from here to the theater." I would plead with the girls who were reluctant to get into an area that was pretty dirty in the first place. We resolved the dirt problem by placing a nice, soft, clean blanket on the bottom of the trunk and show it to the girl of that evening. We developed a great line to convince a girl to enter the five-minute chamber of potential dirt and danger by saying that so-and-so girl had done it and lived through the process.

One memorable night Boy and I had one of our bazillion double dates in our growing years. This night it was with two lovely girls. We went to the outdoor theater. I don't remember his date's name but mine I remember. It was Kathy Kelly, a blond, bombshell from one of the many Catholic Girl's schools in our area. Kathy was not the typical Catholic school girl of the day. She smoked constantly, talked a mile and minute and was

146

very smart. Better, she liked me. And she held her own in philosophical discourse. She hopped into the trunk with me without a single second's hesitation. So far so good. We started making out as soon as Boy put the trunk lid down. But for some strange reason Boy did not start the car to drive us to the theater.

Me: "Oh Boy…Why doest thou not start thy car?" Yeah, I talked funny, still do, but I was making fun of biblical speech.

Boy: "I can't find my keys!"

Me: "Oh hell! I've got them in my pocket!"

Fortunately, Boy and I both knew Betsy-the-Blue-Bitch's interior intimately. By taking out the back seat's backrest, one could gain access to the trunk…but only with a four or five-inch opening. I hugged Kathy Kelly and told her I would simply hand Boy the keys and we would be off. She was happy with that. She was not told that the handoff would be most delicate because we could not pass the key to each other easily. I had to take the key between my thumb and index finger and pass it through the narrow passage to Boy's hand which was equally squeezed. It would have been very easy to drop it in the exchange. Had we done that, all in the dark of course, who knows what black crevice the key would fall into and we had no flashlight to find it if it did happen. We cautioned each other to be damn careful and started to pass the key. I held on tight as I could until I felt Boy's grip on it. Even then I did not let go. I asked him first if he had a good grip on his end and that I would let go only when and if he said yes. He said yes and we were successful.

Kathy and I had a wonderful relationship. It lasted for the next five years on and off. You might be wondering why I went out with an Irish girl from a local Catholic school if I were such a committed atheist. Well, that's an easy. Kathy was a very attractive, flesh and blood female who liked me. I could care less what she believed on Sundays. Besides, as I mentioned earlier, of my little gang, I was the only one who went to the secular, government, taxed-financed Lakeside. Boy, Malbun, Bar and Billy all went to a local Catholic high school. Thus they had huge connections to Catholic girl's schools and I was the beneficiary of these contacts. Plus I went to school with over 2,000 girls at Lakeside which I gladly shared with my gang. It all worked out splendidly.

I think it might be instructive if I mentioned how I met Kathy Kelly in the first place. Earlier that year Boy and I were at one of the Catholic schools for girls. It was about 11 PM so I climbed on the roof which joined a ledge where I had access to the girl's rooms. I made my way along the ledge and found that I was looking into a room where three or four girls were mumping about in PJ's and robes. I had found the Mother Lode! I knocked on the window and luckily, one of the girls I had known back at St. Barnabas was there.

She laughed and opened the window. The good news? I had found da babes. The bad news? They would not let me in.

There, inside this room were now about six or seven teenage girls talking to Boy and me through the window. Boy had climbed up right after me. There was an especially good-looking blond on the left who engaged me in conversation. She had an outfit on that I don't know how to describe. But I could see her starboard breast clearly because her top was partly open. To a teenage boy that is like lighting a firecracker in front of him. I was highly aware of this but said nothing. "Starboard," as I began to call her, was Kathy Kelly.

On the way home I told Boy about how I had got an eyeful of Kathy Kelly's "starboard" side to be precise. Boy made a big deal of this fact and a week later I was talking to still another girl from that school. The conversation wandered here and there until she asked me, "So did you like "Starboard?" I'm still flinching at how amazed I was. Not only did Boy tell some girl about my lovely sighting but that gossip must have gone about the girl's school and this girl brought it up to me. To Kathy Kelly's credit, she not only acknowledged that she had heard of what Boy said but she thought it was funny.

During football season at Lakeside we used to have sock hops after the football games. It was at one of these casual dances early in sophomore year that I met a freshman girl. She was one of the cutest girls I had ever seen. Her name was Angelina Townsend. She had dark hair, large brown eyes, pure, clear skin and smelled of a unique perfume that I came to identify with her alone, Arpege by Lanvin. She was a Lincoln Middle graduate and lived not too far from Lakeside so I could, and did, walk her home frequently in the next three years. She was highly attractive and had the curves and bumps in all the right places. In the next four years, during and after high school, I took her to many dances, events and shared her life..

I met her parents and brother who was two years older than me. Her parents loved to curl and during the curling season were often engaged in that rare sport. Whisking a broom across the ice to get a stone to go where you want it? How Canadian! Angelina was the ultimate "girl-next-door." She was well brought up and I respected and cared for her. Plus she got along with Boy, Bar and others in my little gang as we spent time together. Angelina was in many respects the perfect Lakeside Girl, well dressed, well groomed, aware, college-bound, liked music and opera and spoke clear standard English. She had one virtue I admired very much. She was not "cliquish." She did not turn her nose up at anyone, instead if anything, she was an empath. She was the opposite of a "Mean Girl."

Angelina and I doubled with Boy and his dates many times. We both referred to her as "AT." This stuck and, over 50 years later we still call her that! Our relationship gradually morphed over my years at Lakeside into a firm and deep friendship. It was romantic for about a year or two but I called that aspect off because I worried about getting too involved at too early an age. This might have been a good decision because to this day, 58 years after I met her, we often speak by phone. We are each married to other people of course but we have a deep friendship that nothing can change.

# Chapter 9 Things REALLY get Going in All Areas

During the summer of 1961 Boy and I made good money cutting lawns all over the suburbs. We used Boy's old car, Betsy the Blue Bitch Buick which had a cavernous trunk. Into that large trunk went my leaf sweeper and a power mower plus rakes and an edger. We would cram these items into Betsy and off we would mump to several lawns each day. I had been doing jobs like this since I was nine and had clients that went way back, but we kept on getting new ones because we did a good job, especially on edging which adds a class touch to a well kept lawn.

This work did great things for both of us. First, it provided us with an honest, healthy method of making money. Second, it started and enhanced the process of becoming men. Boys are dependent upon parents and authority figures. Having our own business and expanding it enabled us to become much less dependent on our parents. We began to make our own decisions about money, how to earn it and how to spend it. Third, we did OK. We were not getting rich but we no longer had to ask our parents for spending or date or gas money. We earned it and learned how hard it was to get, so we became much wiser about careless spending. Fourth, we learned how to make joint decisions quickly so that we did not need to hassle and fight over mere mechanical details.

Our routine consisted of starting with one lawn in the morning and then going directly on to the next and sometimes a third, depending on their size and day of the week. If it rained we goofed off a bit but then had to start cutting right afterwards because we did not want to get backed up. We usually were done by 2 or 3 PM and headed right for the beach where we joined our friends in the constant hunt for babes and fun. I put about 80% of what I earned into the bank ..."for college expenses." I don't know how much Boy saved. Never asked him.

Who was Boy? How did we regard our friendship?

Boy walked into my classroom at St. Barnabas in fifth grade. He was of average height, brown hair, average build, a typical nine-year-old Irish-American kid with blue eyes and a great sense of humor. We quickly became fast friends and since I spoke to him by phone at length, yesterday, we have kept this friendship for 63 years. I think the basis of this friendship is honesty more than anything else. Plus we were able to make each other laugh.

From fourth grade through high school, Boy moved with his family about eight times! I never did find out the precise reasons for this, but it had something to do with Harry and Mary's (his parents AKA: "P's") occupation. They operated a small business. Harry was a "jobber" whatever that means. I guess there are a million different ways of being a "jobber." In their circumstance, Harry and Mary went all over the Chicago suburbs and probably into Chicago itself, selling cosmetics from manufacturers to dime stores, larger stores and anyone who wanted to buy. Boy's home was full of shelves that contained row after row of cosmetics in boxes. Once I discovered the contents of some of these boxes I no longer had any interest in them at all, nor did Boy.

Like me, Boy was the youngest of his siblings. I did not know his older brother but I knew his sister, Connie G., who seemed to me to be on a perpetual hunt for a husband. She finally succeeded at the end of our high school years, about 1963. His siblings did not play a very large part of our friendship. But they were there and probably altered him slightly just as my siblings affected my upbringing.

For ten straight years I shared all my adventures and growing up with Boy. We chased girls and talked about them endlessly. We both sang in various choral and solo roles. We played football, basketball, softball, ice skated and advised each other on the best way to deal with "The "P's" who were constantly getting in our way. We used to sing in Betsy after our double dates. Boy particularly liked "Old Devil Moon" from *Finian's Rainbow* which our opera group at Lakeside had performed recently. We analyzed every issue regarding our dates, in great detail. Yet our conversations over those early years were mostly about the real, immediate actions we were taking or wanted to take. Rarely did we discuss politics or religion or matters of the mind.

Why did I call him Boy? One day we were driving in Betsy with his mother Mary to go to a grocery store. As we left the store, Mary, who was sitting on the right side of the car, stuck out her arms and summoned a grocery clerk by waving her hands up and down like a rich dowager in a black and white movie would summon a servant. She cried out, "Boy! Oh Boy!" I've forgotten *why* she wanted to speak to him. All that I remember were the hands going up and down and her imperious "Oh Boy!" I had some other nickname for him earlier but Boy stuck the longest and we still use it.

Later, when Boy and I were alone, we discussed his mother's awkward but very funny summoning of the grocery clerk. I imitated her tone of voice and her hand waving. For the next few weeks whenever I met Boy I would turn my head slightly up and wave my hands up and down bending them at the wrist and recite, "Oh Boy!" This became our shtick of the month and it gradually became our names for each other. We now have called each other "Boy" for over 50 years. Plus we add in the imperial tone of voice.

That summer I was going with Dottie Walsh, a slender blond from the East Coast who stayed with relatives in our town. One day she was hanging at my neighbor's house, My neighbor, Loco Foco, was two years younger than me. (Loco Foco you ask with upturned eyebrows? Yes! That's exactly what we called him.) I knew for some reason there were no parents in his house so I wanted to get her out of there. It just so happened that it was the rare day that I had a car for my use so I drove over to the front of the house and boldly walked in without ringing the bell. I walked into the room where Dottie and my neighbor were talking and gently took her right hand in my left and smoothly pulled her onto my shoulders in a Fireman's Carry. Holding her carefully but tightly I walked out of the room, out of the house and deposited her into my car.

As we drove off I could hear Loco Foco complaining and asking if I intended to bring her back. Happily, she thought this was one big, romantic move which she was the subject of, making it all the better. My first abduction, a la *Seven Brides for Seven Brothers*, was a success. (*Seven Brides for Seven Brothers* was a 1954 musical comedy starring Howard Keel and Jane Powell where all seven brothers abduct their girl friends and take them beyond the pass for the winter.) A year later I would try another Howard Keel style abduction with another girl but it was *not* a hit. I'll describe that in Chapter Ten.

More ideas began to circulate in my little brain that summer. My father was frequently drunk and acted foolishly, causing me to question how one established the ability to justly hold power over another human being. To me cops, teachers, politicians and government bureaucrats were all merely derivative power holders. In other words they used power because someone else somehow "gave" it to them. Usually, it was held that "we the people," through voting, gave them this power. I

157

was suspicious of this as I was not clear on how "majorities" somehow acquired the right to order others around. Clearly dictators, kings and 'heads of State' were frauds in my book.

On a larger and more general level, what was the source of right and wrong in the first place? I had yet to read Socrates, Adam Smith, Thomas Paine or Ayn Rand. The Bible, in which I had had six years of training, was a complete ethical joke which had been so cherry-picked that it was totally useless to me as any rational guide to ethics. I had bumped into Thomas Jefferson and found the Declaration of Independence a moving document. I made serious consideration and comparison of the world's major ethical philosophies much later in my life, after the Army, while I was at the university. Until then the Golden Rule seemed to be enough.

In August of 1961, the summer before my Junior year at Lakeside, I became eligible for the football team again. We had a tradition at Lakeside where we would start our own practice at a local public park system about three weeks before school started, without coaches, equipment or any Lakeside supervision at all. I observed my peers. They had continued to grow larger and stronger but so had I. I wanted to make the team and play the game because I liked its physicality and spirit. Football tests one's courage, especially when you face monsters who are much larger than you.

On about the third day of these informal practices, I was mumping along with my friends at Lakeside Field when I noticed that both my father and mother were standing on the sidelines. This was most odd; in the past my father had shown up for my games but never for a mere practice. And on this day both of "The P's" were there. What was up?

I walked over to them and asked what brought them to my practice. They minced no words. "We've decided to pay for orthodontics for your front teeth. It's going to cost $1,200 and it will make your chewing much more efficient and healthy and you will look better too" intoned my father. Why had they waited until I was almost 16 to do this? Most kids had braces when they were 10 to 12 years old. On the other hand, people had made fun of me all my life for having extended front teeth. They called me "Bucky Beaver".

I asked why they decided to come all the way to Lakeside Playfield to tell me this? Couldn't this have waited until dinner tonight at our home? There was a dramatic pause. My father told me that these braces would affect me positively for the rest of my life and they were not willing to risk spending all this money on them if I had another encounter with a low tackle, causing me to lose more teeth. He was referring to the tackle I had made freshman year which caused me to chip my incisor. He had me there logically. "So we will not sign off for you to play football again at Lakeside."

I was crushed. I don't think they had any notion of how much this decision, *not* allowing me to play football would also affect me the rest of my life. High school football is not easy. You have to really work hard at it to get any good. You have to show up on time, day after day, do the hated wind sprints, endure the injuries, minor and serious, all of which I was very willing to do. But doing all this stuff faithfully encourages a boy to learn internal discipline and to be able to work with others for a common goal. All of this down the tube for braces?

I left the practice field at that moment with my parents. One of my ethical questions had been answered to some degree of clarity. They fed, housed and clothed me, something I was not prepared to do on my own yet. Therefore they had the right to order me not to play football. It was that clear cut. I think in some ways I was hurt by their choice. I certainly felt that way but there was no concrete method of proving my point. I could not know the future. I was a big, strong kid and a practiced wrestler. No one ever hassled me. Football would make me a bigger and stronger kid but who knew what else? What bonds football would forge would *not* be forged. We had no notion of how their absence would affect me.

As I grew up I saw my father drunk on numerous occasions. He would not walk in the door drunk. He would drink himself into various states of incapacity at home. Bruno, the eldest, used to find his booze bottles and pour them out. But that did no real good because my father would just buy more. When he was liquored up he would get on the phone, what Zombie called "Telephonitis," and speak to relatives in a slurred voice. His favorite line seemed to be, "Hey, aunt so-and-so, how are your bowels?" He did not get violent. He would eventually fall asleep. Although he was alleged to have pushed Zombie down the stairs once while drunk but I did not witness this. The really bad vibrations came from my mother who would scream at him. Many a night I can remember the reverberations of her screams going up and down my spine as I lay upstairs in my bed.

I made the vow to forever be a tee-totaler; to *not* become my father. I kept that pledge with three brief exceptions in my later teenage years and once in the Army. But never after that. I never touched hard booze again and am happy to have done so. I'm always in control; booze is expensive and everyone knows I don't drink. I'm always the designated driver.

Weeks later I entered my Junior year at Lakeside not knowing what I would do with all the free time given me by not playing football. They say "The devil finds work for idle hands."

Junior year I skipped the opera which I was eligible to do for the first time and performed in *Prodigy Largess* in which I had a larger role to perform. In fact I was given a short solo which was recorded, a record which I still have. While taking part in musical events I discovered a warren of bathrooms and practice rooms underneath the stage. This provided me with still another venue for smoking and potentially getting in trouble.

Lakeside High School had an employee who seemed to have a full-time job trying to ferret out students who were smoking on school grounds. We called him "Smokey," a dark, serious and troubled looking individual who always seemed to be on the verge of crying. I had a four-year game with him. He never caught me once. It was all due to the efficient design of Lakeside's ventilation system. Lakeside was a huge school in the early '60's. My class had 992 students and it was the smallest! I went to an institution in a very large facility which could hold over 4,000 students, faculty, and staff in one giant, extended building. It had to warmed in the winter and ventilated all the time.

The vents were my secret which I learned to take great advantage. The bathrooms had large vents, a good twelve inches by twelve inches which sucked air out. We tested the suction and found it very potent. I would light up a cigarette sitting on a toilet and a friend would stand out where the water basins were and see if he could smell smoke. For the most part he couldn't. Which meant neither could "Smokey" if he came poking around. Besides, if he did walk into the john while I might be smoking, all I had to do was flush the cigarette down the toilet and pop a piece of gum in my mouth and hang for a while. If he started insisting on inspection I could accuse him of being a total pervert. Given the vast size of the building with its four floors and numerous bathrooms scattered all over the place, I stood a good chance he would never catch me smoking in a john with those great vents pulling out my exhalations. In fact, he never did and I was never caught.

For most of my first two years at Lakeside I was content to smoke in the vented johns. But junior year I discovered those wonderful vents were in many other places too. The stage was rarely used *during the day* and powerful vents were in bathrooms underneath. I found a little alcove in one and set up my "Home Suite" complete with my shaving gear and cigarettes. I also found that the showers had several vents. One of them was around a corner where the coaches did not go and could not even see into. Thus I found that I could have a cigarette in the shower and when I was done the butt went into the toilet and I took a longer, more relaxed shower. Other kids saw me doing this but never squealed on me.

The best smoking place I found was in a classroom. About the middle of junior year I had an English class which not only had a large vent on one side wall toward the floor but it was pretty close to a seat which I managed to get. The seating in that particular room was not the normal arrangement with rows of seats all in front of a teacher's chair and desk. This one was set up in a relaxed, informal group of long, curved tables that formed a semi-circle where the teacher sat at one end. I found out that if I leaned back just a few inches my face and most of my body was out of sight of the teacher because my peers sitting in the semi-circle would be in the way.

Remember In Chapter Two I recalled Jane Montgomery at the skating rink in about third grade who touched my arm? Well, Jane was in this class with the semicircular table/desk arrangement. She sat exactly opposite me on the other long side of the table. She could see me completely no matter how much I leaned back. After class started and we were in discussion I leaned back and lit a cigarette, covering the click of my lighter with a slight cough. The teacher who gave me good grades in that class could not see me as I did this. Then, using the edge of the vent as an ashtray, I leaned forward again after a puff and again appeared on the teacher's periphery so from his prospective, all was normal. Then every so often I would lean back, oh so casually, and take more puffs, blowing the smoke into the vent. The teacher was none the wiser but Jane looked at me in amazement. "How could you do this?" her face said. Better, it also said, "Why can't I do it too?" She had been a cheerleader at Lakeside and I always had a slight crush on her.

I was a naughty boy, a term my mother would have used to describe a kid who was misbehaving but not truly hurting anyone or doing anything really mean. I used to rationalize my behavior on grounds that I was not out to deliberately hurt anyone. I remember lighting a cigarette in a bathroom, walking out into a hallway with hundreds of kids and teachers walking between classes with the cigarette cupped in one hand, books in the other. I would go up to a locker near my study hall that I knew to be unused, place the lighted cigarette on the top shelf inside, and then carefully insert a Cherry Bomb into the end away from the lit part. I had tested this at home and found it took anywhere from six to up to eleven minutes for the fire to gradually burn down to the Cherry Bomb's wick.

After this I would walk into my study hall and casually read a book. I was always worried that somehow the smoke from the lit cigarette would waft out through the slits in the locker door and someone would discover this only to open the door and have the Cherry Bomb go off in their face. I would wait impatiently as the minutes went by. I think I did this about three times in my junior year until I get bored with it. Eventually the fire burned down to the wick and suddenly a huge explosion would ensue, made more intense because of our sitting in a very quiet study hall.

Then there would be running in the hall and wild speculation among my peers. I was never caught and those who knew it had to be me never squealed either.

I had a variation of the Cherry Bomb-in-the-locker shtick. The central staircase in the middle of the school was four stories of steps surrounded by tile and hard surfaces. In the middle of this arrangement was an open area about two feet wide by eight feet long. For four years I frequently walked up or down this staircase with my fellows. Junior year I found another use for my Cherry Bombs by waiting until most of the people using the staircase were out and on their way to class. Then I would stand on the top floor and light a Cherry Bomb and drop it down the exact middle, in-between the stairs. It usually took several seconds to drop and hit the bottom and blow up there. I was on the top, already on my way out of the staircase when it went off. Again pandemonium and people running around not knowing what had happened.

My life at age 16 was not all mischief and girls. Underneath a probing, even intellectual grasping mind was growing. Part of it dealt with music and literature. At 16 I wanted to be a jet pilot and an opera star at the Met. Eventually I did become a pilot but never an opera star. One of these areas of interest I developed in Junior year. All students at Lakeside had to write *The Junior Theme*, a mandatory English requirement for graduation. It was to be a major project requiring proper library research, how to outline and how to end up with a fully thought out major paper on an important subject.

Many of my friends quaked in their boots at the idea of having to write such a mammoth paper and did not look forward to junior year for this very reason. But being a voracious reader all my life, I had no such qualms. I also lucked out because when I finally was required to write *The Most-Important-English-Paper-in-the-History-of-the-World*, *The Junior Theme*, I happened to have one of my best English teachers who actually liked me. I asked him if I could do my theme on Tchaikovsky and how to test the current popularity of his compositions, both in the US and worldwide. He said yes!

Many of my male friends had no enjoyment at having to do library research. I happened to love libraries and had been hanging out in them and knew how to use the card system to look up stuff since I was 12. I had frequently looked up football greats and certain jet fighter pilots. Anyway, at Lakeside we had a standard library with all the usual books but we also had an "AV room" where one could listen to opera, symphonies or even lectures on records. I discovered this oral bonanza freshman year and spent many of my happiest hours listening to one great piece of music after another in that "AV room." I remember with perfect clarity when I first heard Tchaikovsky's *Sixth Symphony*. The records were often old monophonic disks from the 40's and 50's but this Tchaikovsky happened to be one of the early stereophonic records. Our class periods were divided into segments of 40 minutes. I sat down in the "AV room" with this special stereophonic Tchaikovsky *Symphony No. 6, the Pathetique*, about ten minutes into the period.

As I listened with earphones I was swept away at the sheer beauty and magnificence of this piece. About the middle of the third movement, I vaguely remember the bell ringing to change classrooms at the end of the period. I was so thrilled and moved by this piece that I ignored the bell and just listened in a great heaven of emotion. The last movement is a long cry of death and good bye. I was so moved by it I began to cry real tears, not like your girlfriend died but light lacrymal emissions rolling down my cheeks.. (If you want evidence of this supreme emotional moment, go to your computer and type in this:

https://www.youtube.com/watch?v=3ebQYH6EpJ8

It's the Fourth Movement of *Tchaikovsky 6.* on YouTube. One of the many comments about this Masterpiece on YouTube was,

*"Possibly the most gorgeous thing I've ever heard in my life -- an aching, desperate exclamation of hope in the face of futility, the culmination of an entire life and all its joys and sorrows, all cobbled together into a final cry before, at last, it finally fades. Heartbreaking on all levels and bittersweet to the very end. Nothing else compares."*
Writer Unknown

I agree with this summation. I was staggered emotionally by the time the symphony was over. The bell had long since rung and I got in trouble for being late to my next class. When I was asked why I was late I told the precise truth and was laughed at by my peers who overheard my answer to the teacher of the next class. They did not understand my answer. The teacher however, did. He smiled and let it go at that. Needless to say, for the rest of junior year and all of senior year I listened to every bit of Tchaikovsky I could find in that "AV room." And a whole lot of opera too.

P.I. Tchaikovsky

I wrote my Junior Theme on Tchaikovsky. I still have it. I remember the method I used to establish its popularity. I did not consult polls or opinion pieces; instead I found documents of major symphony orchestras around the globe. I remember looking up orchestras in England, Germany, the US, Israel, Japan and even Australia. All of them played the Tchaikovsky Six frequently, so frequently as to establish a pattern of world dominance. Tchaikovsky conquered the world as no general ever could with an army. He conquered my soul, my very being and I have never gotten over him. Nor would I try. The Junior Theme became

171

just another piece of writing for me as I wrote other papers, scripts and monologs in my career, but I never forgot it. I got a very high grade for my paper.


Turning to another form of entertainment we did in the winter. We skitched! We would hang about at stop signs when there was sufficient snow on the ground; when a car stopped we would grab the rear bumper and as the car started down the road we would slide along on our boots in the snow. To do this efficiently we needed good, strong boots and we found the perfect item. They were called engineer boots. They were black, large, with a very firm sole and about an inch-thick heel. We called them hood boots because they were all black and the toughs used to wear them. We convinced our parents that they would be perfect for us because they would last forever and keep our feet warm. Eventually most of my friends and I had them i and we skitched up a storm with them.


We had contests, who could get the longest ride, who could do the most tricks while on the back of a car or truck. I loved it and had a blast finding new places to get a good grab on a car or truck and then warping my way down the road. Part of the fun was that it was dangerous, especially when you might hit a patch of freshly plowed street and have no snow to slide on. Also it was against the law. You had to make sure that a cop did not see you when you started or when the car turned onto a new street. You had to abort very quickly and dive into a snowbank or hide behind one while the cop drove by.

Oddly, I remember in one musical show I did at Lakeside we did a fabulous dance to "Hava Nagila" the popular tune played at Jewish weddings. All the boys, about twenty of us, wore hood boots and made a strong effort to bang them down on the stage floor in rhythm to the music. It had a very dramatic effect and was lots of fun.

We also started to hop trucks. That began after we saw movies where street urchin kids would hop trucks and throw out anything of value inside them as the truck went along and then hop off and try to collect on the side of the street what they threw off. We did not try to steal stuff but we did hop trucks for easy transport. One afternoon after school I hopped a dump truck that had a good size load of dirt in the back. My friends of both sexes would congregate at a local cafe in the late afternoon and as the truck I was riding in came up to this point I decided to do a little guerrilla theater. I pretended to be a Roman general returning to Rome in my horse-driven chariot after a giant, victorious battle. I stood on the dirt holding on to the truck's side with my left hand and thrust my other arm out and up in a 45 degree angle like a victor, Miklos Rozsas' *Ben Hur* music in my mind. The only thing missing was a large, blue cape blowing in the wind. I knew my friends would all see me and they did. The truck conveniently slowed down halfway up the next block so I hopped off and joined my gang which was in stitches at my *Roman Victory Entry Shtick*.

1961 was the year I acquired a used tuxedo for recitals and dances. I found this a frequent uniform for the kind of singing we were doing on and off school grounds. We also wore a white, long-sleeve sweater which was our uniform for more informal singing. I applied for and was invited to join the "Senior Singers" which constituted about 30 dedicated and able vocalists ranging from tenor to baritone to bass. Dr. Jack directed this group and I was his devoted admirer my junior and senior years at Lakeside. It was in this group that I made a life-long friend. "Stevie D. Wonder O", at least that is what I called him after the popular singer of the era. (I'll have lots more to say about Stevie Wonder in the next chapter.)

It was in the Senior Singers as a junior that I learned a lesson of life. I was placed right next to one of the better singers, a bass who had sung as a lead in the

174

opera as a junior. I thought, "How cool, we might even be friends! This guy is truly a BMOC." (Big Man on Campus) It turned out that this great singer, this BMOC, this guy with the melodic voice was one of the dullest guys I ever met. He was truly a drone. He had the personality of an old tree trunk and the wit of a pile of dirty socks. I learned that not only one must not judge a person by a few aspects, but the only honest, genuine way to be was to be yourself; imitation of another was always doomed to flounder.

On the home front, my parents were getting on. They started to receive magazines like "Harvest Years." They were both funny, caring and out-of-it. My father was frequently drunk, but for the most part he was careful about it. He did not jeopardize his job by drinking and driving too much. Most of his extreme drinking was done at home and my mother would shriek at him. My mother amazed us with really famous lines; such as when she was speaking on the phone to a friend, "Have you seen that awful *Elvin* Presley?"

I think at this time I had more of my music-loving friends over to my house. My parents thought I could catch homosexuality by merely hanging around "homos." This was evidenced by sometimes very awkward questions at home about

175

who my friends went out with and did they have girlfriends. I know they suspected me which was a joke because I'd been chasing babes since I was about twelve. One night I happened to have two teenage girls with me and it got late and they needed to get home. I told them I would sneak my old man's car out of the garage and drive them home. While in the act of doing this my father caught me...with the two babes pushing the car out of the garage. I could tell he was happy that I had girls there instead of boys. He offered to drive them home and was most jocular and charming to them. On the way home after we had dropped them off I thought all hell would break loose for attempting to use his car without permission but he never said a single word to me about it! I guess he thought that his last child was straight after all and he was happy about it.

In addition to appearing like old fogies, my "P's" had another interesting diversion. While not hardcore political activists, they did follow politics and held political beliefs. Except, perhaps to my long time benefit, my parents held *opposite* political philosophies! My mother was an Eleanor Roosevelt-loving, long time Democrat, weeping, humanitarian liberal. FDR could do no wrong in her eyes. My father, on the other hand loved President Taft, held that taxation was legalized theft by the government and voted for the Republican presidential candidate every four years.

176

My "P's" would get in my father's company car, drive to the polling station in our home town and vote opposite. I would ask them why bother, didn't their votes cancel each other out? They had no answer to this except mumbling something about voting was a duty. Was it? Later I examined this carefully.

My benefit from this apparent parental chaos was that I emerged without strong ties to either position which allowed me to gradually judge politics on my own grounds, from the values I evolved. I did not have strong political beliefs until I was out of the Army and took philosophy and political science at the university. I had gradually formed some rudimentary political beliefs by then. These beliefs were formed in grammar, high school , early college and by observing the world and reading. I had grown up right after the most obnoxious, killing spree in human history, also known as World War II. Marxist Communism was a monstrous bloodbath and still is. Fascist regimes were no better. Both involved the use of the secular State to kill, maim and starve millions of human beings. Democratic states were only slightly better.

It was a democratic state which dropped the first two Atom Bombs killing hundreds of thousand of men, women and children indiscriminately. Before that,

177

General Curtis LeMay managed to kill even more Japanese men, women and children with his low-level fire-bombing of many major Japanese cities that were made mostly of wood. This hastened the end of WWII with the Japanese. The GI's who were ready to invade the Japanese Homeland itself were very grateful to Truman who approved it. No surprise then that I became a Libertarian in about 1969 and still am 50 years later.

In the spring of '62 John Beard, my associate who nipped the stolen wine and hid it in my treehouse lair, had a new scheme. This time he was in love. The girl was very popular, rich; a concert pianist in our class who didn't know he existed. I advised him to do something very quickly of a significant musical nature. But he had never stepped into our musical world in any respect in his three years at Lakeside. He was tone deaf and cared less about opera, symphonies or piano music.

He had a super fix though. He knew her large brown house had a long, curved driveway that entered a private road where cars were required to stop because there were lots of bushes that obscured entry to the larger road. He knew she would have to stop at that point to leave her place. He knew this because I had de-

178

scribed her place in great detail to him, having been to her home on several occasions to practice music.

He planned to find out when she would be driving from her home in the early evening at dark, wait at the private road and as she began to enter the private road, kick the side of her car, cry out loudly as if he had been struck by it and lie there. He would feign pain when she saw him on the ground. Out of massive guilt she would take him into her car and back down the driveway to her home. Once in there, on a couch under a blanket, John would win her over with his charm and suave. All he needed from me was to show him where she lived.

A week or so later John found out she would leaving her home in her car at about 7 PM, dark enough to accomplish his *love plan*. Curious to know if he had the chutzpah to actually go through with this idiocy, I showed him where she lived and waited with him in the bushes for her to drive out in her car.

Surprisingly, we did not wait long; she came out in her brand new car, nice and slow, stopping at the private road. This is where John's *Love Plan* began to unravel, It was now up to him to swiftly move two paces and kick her car on the side, cry out and fall on the ground. He began to move but instead of lunging with his foot for her car, he began to literally tremble, his whole body shaking in fear. By the time he had worked up the nerve to do the kick she had slowly and carefully pulled out into the private road and was gone. He had completely blown the *Love Plan!*

He was unconsolable. He knew it was all his fault and didn't say much for the next two weeks. I thought of all the screwy plans I had made and screwed up in the last sixteen years. He appreciated my silence about his really funny episode in the bushes and thanked me for not making fun of him,

Another incident took place later that year. Angelina Townsend, (A.T., we called her.) and I, went on a day trip together one lovely day. It was a canoe trip down a nearby water system, down a stream that drained it southward and to a point exactly 100 yards from Boy's current pad. Not wanting to overshoot, I had placed a marker on the spot where I had to beach the canoe in order to go to Boy's for lunch. We planned this to a T, estimating how long it would take to paddle down the system, portage around a spillway, and then paddle down the little stream to the point near Boy's.

This was a good forty years before everyone carried cell phones so Boy had to arrange his side of the lunch to take place within a plus or minus time portal. Once on the water no communication was possible. The plan worked perfectly. AT and I placed the canoe into the water, paddled across a little lake, portaged the spillway making our way down to the marker. The marker was still there! Everything had worked out as planned. After beaching the canoe we walked the hundred yards and had a great lunch at Boy's pad. Then we reversed course and went back to where we had started. Then I drove A.T. home. She arrived back home about 4 PM and I returned the canoe to its owner and back home by about 5:30 PM.

This is when my mother created "The Ban List!" For some reason, I've forgotten why, I was gone longer than I should have been or I did not tell my parents what I was doing at all that day, whatever it was. My mom, the Great Zombie, called up A.T. at about 4:30 that afternoon and asked her if she knew where I was and had she seen me today. A.T., not wanting to get me in any trouble and knowing all I had to do before I got home was to return the canoe, told her that she had not seen me and did not know where I was. She obviously lied, but she did so to protect me.

When I got home a short time later, unaware that Zombie had called A.T., I was asked where I had been. I told the truth and described a lovely day canoeing and having lunch at Boy's pad. This honest admission turned AT into a major liar and Zombie declared that A.T. was now and forever on The Ban List. What was that I wanted to know. Well it was just a list of people I should not ever deal with because of their low character. A.T. was the only person ever put on The Ban List and it was quickly forgotten. Shortly over a year later, Zombie had no problem calling up A.T. when Zombie wanted A.T. to intercede for her in a scheme she had about me. A.T. did it but she had her own motives which were more out of curiosity and loyalty to me. In the end The Ban List was forgotten. Although A.T. was completely bewildered by it.

# Chapter 10 Senior Year & Graduation

By the summer of 1962, I was sixteen and about to be a senior at Lakeside. My friends and I continued our tradition of D-Nights. Although by then we all had driver's licenses and access to cars. The things we did in cars! I've already written about sneaking into drive-ins in the trunk of Boy's Betsy the Blue Bitch Buick. But another long-time friend, Bar, had a Volkswagen Beetle. When I first met Bar in the early grades of St. Barnabas, he lived directly on the route I used to walk to school. He lived in a large, multi-story home and had a cat which seemed to come and go with ease, climbing up to the roof, walking along ledges and entering the house through various windows.

Bar was an interesting contradiction. He was not a tall, athletic type. He was not an actor or musician in school. He always had a girlfriend. Boy and I wondered for years about *how* Bar attracted the girls. He was an Irishman through and through. His hair was dark brown, his face, at least to Boy and I, seemed to have a very slight Oriental look to it. This was an amazing thing because he had not a drop of Chinese or Japanese or any other kind of Asian blood in him. He was famous for driving along in his Beatle with a girl in his arms, kissing her full faced on the lips and holding her there as he drove along. I witnessed this more than once. He was not a rich guy. Boy and I were stumped as to how he was so successful with the babes. When a girl was with Bar she seemed to be mesmerized by him. He could do no wrong from their point of view. Boy theorized that it was his soft hands that did it. We joked that he had soft, puffy hands and that somehow these hands caressed their way to all the girls' hearts. He constantly made models, ships, cars, planes; Bar had great hand motor skills all through grammar school.

He had two other virtues which I think were really his romantic secrets. He was always very smart and got very high grades, both at St. Barnabas and at the Catholic high school he and Boy went to. I think he was introspective to a great degree and the results of his brains and his thoughtfulness gave him an awesome personal confidence which most teenage boys lack. I believe this was his secret and whether or not he was aware of its power, he had more dates, more girls trying to get his attention, more amore in general than Boy and I combined ever had. We were jealous of him in this respect but since he was not a blowhard about it, since he remained a loyal friend to both of us, we simply watched him with awe and tried to be like him to some degree. Bar eventually worked his way through dental school and became a dentist. Then he went into a huge debt and became an Endodontist. We joked that when he joined an endodontic team on the West Coast about $76,000 in debt, after his third patient he would be in the black and remain there for his whole career.

Another solid Irishman joined our little gang freshman year in high school. We called him Rocco. He was tall and thin with very fair, clear skin and he too was very bright. He was a cousin of one of my great former unrequited flames (One of many who did not reciprocate my ardor!!) Mary O'Sullivan. Rocco had been brought up somewhere in the South but he had not a trace of a southern accent. What he did have was a love of what he called, "*Spirituals*, good old singing for God." He described going to large camp gatherings where blacks would sing for hours, swaying and moving to the songs. He heard every "Spiritual" ever written and he loved them all.

When Rocco learned that I was a very rare guy who wanted to be an opera singer, he became a great fan of mine, at least in terms of begging me to sing "Spirituals" for him. I would do so, at least the few I knew. He loved it and demanded more, not because I sang them well, but that I did them just for him! I would launch into an *a cappella* rendition of "Sometimes I Feel Like A Motherless Child"* and Rocco would melt. I had learned the song from Paul Robeson singing it on an old, 78 RPM record my parents had which I played on their very old, wind-up gramophone. It was a good song that I liked and it had a bass range so I could handle the high and low notes easily. One summer evening on a D-night, Rocco, Bar, Boy and I were lying in the grass at a small public park near the Lake Michigan talking about those things that interest 16 year olds. We were a bit older than the kids in the movie *Stand By Me* but we had that easy, straight forward conversation that old friends share. We did not do anything special that night but I shall always remember it as one of the emotional high points of these night forays because it was so peaceful, so right, so appropriate for our age group.

*Want to hear Paul Robeson sing "Sometimes I Feel Like A Motherless Child?" Click on this:  <<u>https://www.youtube.com/watch?v=KiJx1Hbn_KM</u>>

During the summer before senior year I finally had my first introduction or partially successful attempt, at making love with a girl. She slept out on a screen porch and invited me to join her. She was a knockout blond, smelled like Old Spice and was about a year younger than me. It was not a perfect, totally complete, uninhibited sexual union. Instead it was a series of slow but more intimate moves on both our parts. I walked home afterward, climbed the tree next to our home with three, very well-practiced movements, descended onto the roof, walked up to the chimney and had my *almost dawn cigarette*, before climbing over to my dormer and entering my bedroom and falling asleep about five AM.

That morning exactly six hours later I got a phone call from Boy:

Oh Boy!

Yah? I'm a bit sleepy.

Last night I woke up at 3 AM and I felt a certain event was happening. Did you finally do it with her?

Oh Boy. I don't believe in mental telepathy.

You *did* do it! I know you did! I want details! I knew you did it at 3 AM.

Oh yeah? How?

I don't know how. I'm just certain you did! I felt it.

187

And on that conversation went. He was certain. I, leery that some sibling might hear me, was reluctant to talk details. Neither one of us believed in mental telepathy. I later pieced together how Boy *knew* I had done it. He was certain because he knew in advance I was going over to her pad and that she had invited me. When he heard I was still sleepy at 11 AM the next morning he concluded that I had been with her most of the night in that screened porch. He did not need to jump to any conclusion because what I did was what every teenage boy wants to do, what *he* wanted to do. So by saying that he *knew I did it,* he was just trying to get me to admit or deny it.

My parents, now had to only feed three kids, the other two having flown from the nest. Since my aunt and grandmother passed, they decided to rebuild our kitchen. More accurately. it was to be gutted and a whole new kitchen, new floors, new walls, new appliances, everything would be replaced. The process took about two full weeks in which we had to go out for dinner every night. We went to one restaurant after another, American food, Mexican food, Italian food! I think we even went to a Chinese restaurant once.

We went to middle class places. One day on a major truck route we went to a place that could only be called a *dive* for truckers. I think after looking through the menu, we all ordered cheeseburgers and fries, thinking that all the other stuff could not possibly be any good considering the drab walls, the rather slutty waitress and the drunks at the bar. Pendron and I found that the men's bathroom, was not only dirty but had a prophylactic vending machine in it, a sure sign that this place was a major dive.

When our burgers arrived we were amazed at how good they were. The fries were hot and tasted delicious and my parents loved the coffee. When we left we we had to admit our prejudice toward the place *before* we tried it. Yes, it looked like a dive but the food was so good that this truck stop was the only restaurant we visited twice in that fortnight. In other words, *Don't judge a restaurant by it slutty waitresses or dirty bathrooms!*

While I had been theorizing about the nature of music for most of my life, by the time I was ready for my senior year at Lakeside I began to explore the physics of music. I asked many questions, the primary one being, Why is music so emotional? How does it burst through the intellectual side of human beings and thrust directly to the heart or the emotions? In order to understand and attempt to answer this question still more basic questions had to be asked. What is music, how is music distinguished from noises or traffic sounds? I suppose if I had taken a course in music for an instrument, I would probably have worked out all this stuff five years earlier by reading textbooks that dealt with these primaries. But I never had. I sang my way through school.

Music consists of sound vibrations, specific vibrations at specific pitches. If you ever listen to an orchestra warm up, the concert master stands, the orchestra silences, he then signals for the oboist to play an A. Then the orchestra all match their instruments with that A. That A is played at 440 Hertz. So music takes these pitches and plays them in a sequence which is usually called a melody. Now we have notes and melody. Then we have drums which help accentuate things with great rhythmic drama and before you know it, when you add in the rhythm of these sounds and the bits of silence in-between them and the dynamics of the notes...how loud or soft they are played, you end up with a piece like *Twinkle Twinkle Little Star.* Add in still more esoteric elements and you have a Beethoven Symphony or, if you add in the human voice, a Verdi opera! Now you have something supremely nice!

But *why* is it nice? Why did the particular notes, silences, melodies and dynamics of Beethoven or Mozart or Verdi become world-wide favorites whereas some of the minor composers are perhaps remembered for one popular piece or even forgotten? Why was Mozart so obviously a hundred times better than Salieri? I began searching for the answer to these questions about age twelve. By age 16 approaching senior year in high school I had thought about this over and over, adding a little new data each year but I never found a definitive answer. I'm 73 as I write this and I *still* don't know! Oh surely there have been many theories based on this or that. But when you examine them carefully they break down and lead to no real answers. There are musicologists who maintain some very highfalutin theories, but if you can understand them they are really only saying *if, maybe, possibly*. In the end they have no unassailable answer.

I remember reading one musicologist who wrote that certain rhythms were enjoyed by humans because they mimicked the beat of the heart. Even baby elephants were susceptible to these rhythms because they were like their elephant

191

mother's heart beats which babies could hear and feel. That's fine as far as it goes but how does that account for the frenetic rhythm one finds in the works of Igor Stravinsky who changed symphonic music forever with his *Firebird*? Or any of the alleged music which was called "Heavy Metal?"

Senior year began with the announcement that the Opera Group would be doing *Guys and Dolls* so we gradually began to learn that grand show. But before *Guys and Dolls*, we had a lighter show to put on in the Fall in which I was offered a good part. In fact, it was the part of my dreams. All my life I had dreamed of singing a romantic duet with a gorgeous soprano and a full orchestra. That Fall, at age 17, I did exactly that. It's a story worth retelling.

One of the most beautiful girls at Lakeside was Maria Costa. She was a tall, gorgeous blond with brown eyes. As a soprano and a junior, she was eligible for Opera Group. She got into the Opera Group and most of the boys' eyes were on her wherever she went, especially mine. So for the Fall show we were cast together as a doctor and his girlfriend and had a great duet to sing together. This show required rehearsals and I found myself over at her house singing with her. She stood about

5'7," a willowy figure with a mercurial personality, one minute attractive and warm to me and the next indifferent. I was completely captivated by her. I wanted to kiss her and embrace her of course. How that happened for the first time is intriguing, baffling, sad and hilarious.

The soloists, after having practiced for several months with piano and chorus accompaniment, were scheduled to sing for the first time with full orchestra about a week before the first dress rehearsal. When Maria and my duet came up we walked onto the stage and looked out. The house lights were up and we could see most of the opera group and other hangers on in the audience. In the pit, was the Lakeside Opera Orchestra with Dr. Jack standing there, baton in hand. This was my senior year; I was 6'1" tall and had sung many solos with Dr. Jack conducting in my years. Yet all I could think about was how much I wanted to kiss this gorgeous babe about to sing with me.

We began; it was about 10:30 in the morning. About half way through the duet. Dr. Jack lowered his baton and stopped the music. He looked up at us standing there about a foot apart as we sang. Dr. Jack said to me, "Ben, you are not acting like this woman is your girlfriend whom you adore. I want you to act more like you are in love with her. I think you ought to kiss and hug her and see if this makes a difference."

*Shazam!* I wanted to kiss and embrace her more than anything in the world and now I was being *ordered* to do so by the director of the show! I walked up to her and very gently kissed and hugged her. Everyone in the whole theater could see me do this. It was such an anti-climatic moment. Maria never mentioned this ordered, stage kiss and embrace; we never discussed it. In the performances on stage several weeks later with a real audience we both blew it. She forgot her lines and I cracked on a high note. I kissed her only one more time, after taking her home after a cast party. We never became lovers.

Chicago was about a half-hour drive from my hometown. Growing up in a suburb was quite different from living in the big city and for the most part I preferred being back home. Chicago was loud, smelly, overcrowded, and a place (for me at least) to visit, but not to stay. As a young boy I remember going to Chicago's Near North side with my parents and standing on Oak Street. There, I embraced one reality of city life. I was looking at the street sign that read "Oak Street" when the most disgusting waft of odor struck me which almost knocked me down. This massive, pungent, revolting odor was not something that was a temporary or fleeting. It stayed there! My parents smelled it too. I asked my father what it was. He replied with two words, "Stock yards." When the wind blew in from the south west it frequently brought with it the vile, stinking smell of the famous Chicago Stockyards as thousands of animals were slaughtered, rendered and prepared to become our "dumburgers" and steaks. That odor was so strong that even after we walked into the building we could *still* smell it. This is one of my first, gross memories of Chicago. Fortunately for the people of Chicago, the stock yards later migrated south to St. Louis and Omaha.

There were other unpleasant memories. I went to a birthday party for one of my St. Barnabas classmates to a Chicago White Sox game about 1954. We parked several blocks from the ball park which was at 35th and Shields. We began to walk toward the park when a small gang of little black kids began to start a fight with us. We were 9 year olds! Why would little black kids want to do this? They were smaller than most of us but they outnumbered us. There were about ten of us; it seemed thirty or more of them. They came at us like little ants, starting to punch us. While my immediate emotion was one of surprise and wonderment, I had no time for thinking because one of the little kids, a good six inches shorter than me, started to take a swing at me. I easily dodged it and we all began to run toward the ball park. The birthday boy's father, who happened to be 6'4, Mr. Connor, then broke it up with loud bellows and his imposing appearance. None of us could figure out why these kids had attacked us, especially when they were so much shorter. Also, we could not figure out their motivations because none of them tried to rob us, in fact they did nothing but start punching. Were we white kids from the suburbs *invading* their territory? Was it solely a race issue? We never found out but it was another negative impression of Chicago.

The next and almost universal part of any large city was the overcrowding. People everywhere, on the streets, in the shops and offices, in restaurants, all talking, yelling, making various noises...too many people at one place and one time for me. Oh how I enjoyed the open spaces of my hometown with its numerous parks, beaches, golf courses. Along with the overcrowding came the constant tumult, pandemonium and occasionally very loud racket. The one constant of Chicago was traffic clamor, honking, squeals, frequent engine noise and truck exhaust. It seemed an emergency vehicle with its blaring siren screamed close or nearby almost constantly.

Another unavoidable part of a big city. You put a lot of people in a small space, this is what happens.

Then there was Chicago's reputation for crime, both in the streets and in politics. The street crime, muggings, hijackings, robberies, murders were legend. As I grew older I realized that Carl Sandberg's "City of Big Shoulders" was also the city of Big Crime. For twenty years I read in the Chicago Sun Times how Chicago's mayor would be embarrassed about the corruption at the highest level in the Chicago Sanitary Commission. The mayor, for most of my memory, was the elder Richard J. Daley who occupied the top crook position from 1955 to his death in 1976. It seemed he must have replaced a corrupt and jailed commissioner every year. But that is all he did. He replaced the corrupt head only for that replacement to be found guilty of some major crime within year or two. People were afraid of walking from their office buildings at the end of the work day to their cars parked in various lots around the city because of roving gangs that would attack anyone and rob them blind. Another major negative strike against Chicago.

But large cities have many positive aspects to offset the negative. Chicago had many good things about it. For me it was the two, world-class, music venues, the Chicago Lyric Opera on Wacker Drive near the river and the Chicago Symphony Orchestra (CSO) on Michigan Avenue not far from the Art Institute. I grew up with these most high places. The only problem was that I could not afford them and they were 18 miles or more from my home.

However I did learn to get around the price problem by regularly attending Ravinia Park Festival concerts in Highland Park way up north. I found a unique way to get in without paying. Ravinia Park is a magnificent venue for orchestra with a huge lawn where people spread blankets and enjoy picnics while listening to the CSO (or pop groups) play. The area itself was surrounded in the '50's and '60's with a stand of trees which covered up the chain-link fences preventing people from sneaking in.

One afternoon I drove up there and looked the wire fence over. I discovered the trees covered many sins. Especially if one had a large, wire-cutter in hand, which I did. The chain link fence stretched across fixed, steel poles which were planted securely into the ground. Between the fixed, steel poles, a thin vertical stretch of wire held portions of the wire fence together. I delicately cut the thin wire in two places. This allowed me to remove the wire I had cut which made an opening about 20 inches wide, just enough to allow me and a date to slip through. Then I reinserted the thin wire back into the fence and the opening was no more and no-one could see that there had been an opening made at all. I named this opening "My Zipper." How did I get the wire cutter from my car into the area? I wrapped it in a blanket, looking like any other Ravinia patron!

Another reason that allowed me to take a date into Ravinia over and over again those early summers in the 60's was that the security force for pop concerts was looking for drunks and sneakers. But on those nights that the CSO played, security was very lax...what teenager would ever sneak into a symphonic concert? I was amazed that over 40 years later I was visiting Angelina Townsend, in Maryland. She showed me a special nicknack that looked very familiar. It was a small hunk of thin wire, maybe two inches long. It was from that wire fence at Ravinia. I had given it to her in the 60's when we had gone to Ravinia for a CSO concert.

There was more. The cost of getting into the park itself was higher than I could afford, the additional cost of sitting in the fixed, covered seats, under the curved roof was even more outrageous. After using my *zipper* to get into the park, I would stand with my date by the inner area where the expensive seats were. I noticed that of 1,500 seats, unless Mozart himself came to conduct, there would always be empty seats due to illness, traffic hazards or other unknown causes. The ushers, mostly college age kids, helped me almost every time I went there. I would say to them, "Say, I noticed that those two seats over there (and would point to them) are empty, would you mind if I took my date and sat in them please?" I was never told no. So in this way I managed to see concert after concert free of charge, usually with a date who went along with my methods.

But I digress. The Chicago Lyric Opera House was not amenable to sneaking in, so I went to it only when friends had extra tickets or when cheap tickets were available. There were two great, world-class museums. The Field Museum had every type of natural animal and specimens to keep naturalists happy for life, and that was only on the first floor. The Museum of Science and Industry was even larger and had so many cool exhibits, from a captured German submarine (U-505) to a whispering gallery, where the mysteries of sound waves were explored. I shall always associate the smell of Pine-Sol, the floor cleaning solution, with this giant museum because when I went there once the floor was being cleaned with it.

Another prodigious positive was the professional sports teams. "Da Bears" were my favorites. For hockey fans there were the Blackhawks and baseball fans could go to see the Cubs lose (which they did for most of my childhood) in the northern part of the city to the American League White Sox in the South part. Famous and prestigious universities and colleges in Chicago were too numerous to name. And if you were a physics geek, you could drive out west of Chicago a few miles to Batavia, to see the Enrico Fermi Institute where they had all sorts of atomic research going on.

Speaking of Chicago, a funny anecdote occurred to Boy and I at Chicago's famous, Soldier's Field. At the end of the football season senior year, somewhere in December when the temperature was hovering about 26 degrees F, Boy and I went to this massive stadium for the annual Catholic V Public high school Championship.

I think that year it was between Fenwick, the Catholic winner and Lane Tech, the government/public winner. There were so many people at that stadium that day we could barely move. I remember talking to Boy about this or that when, somehow, the crowd became so thick that it literally swept him up and out of sight! He was at the time about 5'7," 135 and was carried away by the crowd like an autumn leaf blown across a newly cut lawn. I called and called but the noise that Gargantuan crowd made drowned me out. I finally decided that he would probably go to our designated seats when he was released from the crowd. He *was* finally released and did return to our seats. I don't remember who won the ball game that memorable day. All I remember was Boy being carried away by the crowd.

By senior year at Lakeside I had been hitchhiking for five years or more. I had no car so when my friends were absent or I needed to go somewhere I nearly always hitchhiked. I got good at it because I thought about it and studied it. I got to the point where I think I had mastered it. How? The first issue seemed to me to place myself in the driver's seat of the car which potentially might pick me up. What could I do to make that driver *want to* stop his car, let me in and drive along with me? I concluded that I must look clean cut and non-menacing. Also I would have to place myself in a position on the road where the potential car could stop easily, out-side the major flow of traffic. The result was that I created a list of dos and do nots.

### Do's:

*Dress cleanly so that the driver thinks you will not stink.*

*Look the driver directly in the eye with a calm, upbeat expression.*

*Place yourself in a position so the driver can stop easily such as a stop light or stop sign.*

*Know the geography and streets and precisely where you are going.*

### Do Nots:

*Do not hitchhike on a freeway. Cops will harass you if you do.*

*Do not sit down or look bored or filthy.*

*Do not have an attitude of pain, arrogance or insouciance.*

Eventually I had the art of hitchhiking down to a perfection. It was almost as if I had a driver at my bidding. By the time I was in the Army at age 20 and in uni-form, it was really easy. Not only could I enter military airfields and fly on a space available basis which I did on most of my leaves but getting around on the fields and into the towns was fast when wearing a uniform. I remember once in Honolulu as a soldier I missed the bus back to Fort Shafter from Schofield Barracks after a day at the rifle range. I was hungry and tired and wanted to get back in time to eat dinner at the mess. I was wearing my green Army uniform, highly polished, black boots and, slung over my right shoulder, a magnificent M-14 battle rifle. I walked off Schofield Barracks through the main gate and got out of sight of the gate guards. The third car that came along was a local Japanese guy who picked me up. He was going all the way down the hill into Honolulu. We chatted and he never once mentioned the fact that I was packing major heat in the form of this large rifle. We chatted about all sorts of things and by the time we got to Fort Shafter where I was quartered, he said to me, "Oh what the hell, I've enjoyed our conversation, let me drive you to your barracks." And he did. It probably took him an extra twelve minutes counting going in and out of the base. So efficient was this trip that I beat the bus back to the barracks! I had many other adventures and very funny times hitchhiking across this country. But those anecdotes will have to wait for another time.

Senior year an event happened that reverberates down through time to this very moment 56 years later. Every Fall we had a clothing or canned food drive to help the less fortunate. We went about the community, door to door asking for clothing or canned foods. By the end of the drive we had a dance to celebrate making our goal. The day of the drive at lunch I was asked by one of the very prettiest girls in my class to come over to a friend's home that evening for a "drink or two" before the door-to-door action. She told me who else was coming. It was an impressive list, an all- state fullback, two, very popular and good looking girls and several guys who were National Merit Scholars headed for prestigious, Eastern colleges. It was an invitation to join the "popular clique" for an innocent cocktail party. I thanked the attractive girl standing in front of me but declined on the grounds that I did not drink. I wished her well and urged her to make sure that the driver of the evening had not consumed too much.

That evening after their "cocktail party" about six of them hopped into a car and within minutes one of my classmates was dead, the all-state fullback would never pay football again; one of the kids broke his back and would never walk again and the very pretty girl who invited me to the affair had her face cut grotesquely by shattered glass in the accident. This incident and its graphic mental pictures of horror remain clearly with me to this day. I felt at the time an immense sorrow. I knew all of the kids in that car. I knew the driver very well. He was a competent singer and an excellent scholar but a terrible driver even when sober. Now, when I remember that fatal evening, I still feel the same sorrow . The years may have diminished it but it has never completely gone away. This was also another reason why I have remained  a tee-totaler all my life.


One evening I wanted to speak at length with Maria Costa, the blond soprano who had run over my emotions with her hot and cold attitude toward me. That night I happened to have a car to use. I arranged with several friends to reenact a *Seven Brides for Seven Brothers* style kidnapping like I had done with had Dotty Walsh who had laughed and enjoyed it. That night Maria had gone out with some doofus.  I found it amazing that she had chosen to go out with him at all. My friends and I drove up to within about 80 feet of her home and waited for him to drop her off which he eventually did. While he and Maria were standing in her driveway I walked up to them and casually asked her if I could see her left hand. She was intrigued and offered it to me. I gently took it and pulled it and her arm over my neck and bent down and picked her up easily in a fireman's carry, casually taking her purse and asking her date to watch over it. Then I carried her to my car and began to put her in. My friends had opened the door and managed to place themselves between my car and her date who really did nothing to prevent her abduction.

In my mind I was already thinking ahead to what would happen in Opera Group the next Monday when word of this little escapade got out. It made me laugh hysterically. It was my hysterical laughter that scared Maria. She had not said a word from the moment I slung her over my shoulder and began to put her in my car. But as I began to laugh hysterically she began to tremble and become hysterical herself. Then she began to scream. Not wanting to hurt her in any way I let her go. She ran back to her date, grabbed her purse and walked to her door and disappeared inside. Thus my second attempt at extracting a beautiful girl from another guy went terribly south. All I could do was to get into my car with my friends and slowly drive away.

Oddly, while Maria Costa and I never discussed my little attempt to snatch her away that night, the tale did make fast and quick gossip. The next Monday at Opera Group the buzz was all over. I got the word from Maria's best friend that Maria thought it was "romantic." Lot of good that did me, *after* the fact. She continued to speak to me lovingly one day and ignore me the next. It was after high school I bumped into Maria one day. I asked her if she would like to take a ride over to the beach where I was life guarding and she consented. There, sitting in the sand with her, I told her why I had done the *Seven Brides for Seven Brothers* bit, how much potential I saw in her as a singer and a potential girlfriend and how completely frustrating her hot and cold behavior to me had been all through my senior year. When I told her these things she began to cry, not just tiny sounds but large tears rolled down her face and great sobs racked her which then forced me to gently hold her in my arms. Again, lots of good this did. It was too little too late for another unrequited love.

I would see her around town several more times before I left my hometown for good. But before I did, I hitchhiked down to the college she was attending and spent several days with her. My last moment with her was spent silently holding hands. She seemed to want to tell me a lot more than she did but somehow we both knew that this was not meant to be. After she graduated from college she became a professional singer. Although I talked to her once years later, I never saw her again.

One relationship I realized and cemented senior year was with my singing buddy, Stephen D. Wonder. I nicknamed him that after the blind, pop singer of the day. I met Wonder in freshman year. We were in all the same singing groups as we spent four years at Lakeside. By sophomore year he was leading us in songs now and then. We did not become fast friends until senior year. By senior year we discovered we were kindred spirits in our love of music. We both were in *Guys and Dolls* as principals, he the lead, my part, not so large. We double-dated two of the school's most popular girls; both blonds, both singers and we were on top of our game. Wonder wanted to make a living at music and he did. He went to a very good college for his undergraduate degree in music, then went on to a famous eastern college for a masters in conducting and never looked back. He spent most of his career as the music director and conductor of his own symphony orchestra in Minnesota.

During this time, while I went to college at a state school, learned how to fly light aircraft and spent time in government thrall during Vietnam, he was learning his craft. We kept in touch, compared our lives and the musical experiences we were having. He sent me cassette tapes of some of his conducting experiences with his college orchestra. I sent him reviews of musical greats I saw on stage and my experience performing in a musical while in the Army in the chorus. We keep in touch to this day.

For my final musical event at Lakeside most of my musical friends and I tried out for and were given a full orchestral accompaniment for a solo effort. Some played the piano, others sang, in most cases, arias from well-known operas. It was the traditional *Commencement Concert*, a parade of some of the best singers and players at Lakeside 1963. I loved opera like many of my peers but chose a piece from a broadway musical that had much meaning for me. I chose "This Nearly Was Mine" from *South Pacific* by Rodgers and Hammerstein. I chose it to represent all the girls who I cared for but did not reciprocate. There were many. It represented my intense sorrow for my classmates hurt and killed in that car crash. It represented my ongoing sorrow and confusion at my father's continuing drunkenness. It represented every failure I ever had. I don't wish to convey the idea that I was convinced I was no good. I had my share of successes too. It's just that this song was so incredibly beautiful to me from the first time I heard it in the early 50's.

The Commencement Concert took place on June 6, 1963. 21 seniors delivered arias, songs and concertos accompanied by the Lakeside orchestra. They ranged from Beethoven, to Puccini, Tchaikovsky, Donizetti, Mozart, and in my case, Rodgers and Hammerstein. Wonder, who was a seasoned tenor, sang "Una Furtive Lagrima" from *Elixir of Love* by Donizetti. By this time I was a practiced, vocal soloist with a bass range but I still had not found what opera singers call "place-ment." I was about 6'2" tall, 180 pounds and very healthy. I knew the piece front-wards and backwards. I had worn the hands off my accompanist doing the piece over and over, trying different phrasing, different dynamic accents. So when it came my time to walk on the stage I was ready and able. I sang the piece easily, bowed, Dr. Jack winked and smiled at me when I was done. Then it was over, four years of musical training, four years of musical effort, four years of learning and making friends. If you would like to hear Ezio Pinza sing this piece, here's the link:

https://www.youtube.com/watch?v=4zyi8FV5eTE

The next day my mother told me she thought I sang OK but was very stiff in my movements and my bow at the end. She was probably right. If I had done this in 2018 it would have been recorded by a bazillion cellphones and probably an HD fixed camera and we might have a record of that concert. I wonder if anyone ever made a mere audio recording of that last concert in 1963.

Thus concludes my high school years at Lakeside HS in Illinois near Chicago. I had grown up at that school. When I went to the University of Illinois later I was

211

fully prepared in the musical arena by that experience, led by Dr. Jack. All that summer of 1963 after graduation he gave me personal voice lessons for free, once a week. Finally he told me he had given me all he knew how and gave me the name of another teacher in town... which led to the rest of my life.

# Afterward

I wrote *From Here to Puberty* in seven months in 2018. Boy gave me the idea. We would often reminisce about the old days at St. Barnabas. We could remember so many funny things that happened. He encouraged me to write them down in the form of notes and from that point on it took off. I had such a good time writing down the stories that were true events. I found that the stereotype of an author sitting in front of a blank 81/2 X 11 paper in terror and forgetfulness was not true in my case. The more I laughed the more I wrote.

Even though the growing disillusionment with Catholic theology was a serious and far-reaching event in my life, even *that* had one hilarious anecdote after another to recall. So recall I did, one year after another. I wanted to be factually accurate so I checked with as many of the people in the book as possible. I checked with my siblings over and over, sometimes getting slightly different versions of the same anecdote! On the whole I was usually correct. Since I'm the youngest of my clan, my older siblings usually could remember each anecdote as I presented it but on a few occasions could not remember details.

Then there were the many well-meant suggestions as to how I ought to write this book. Many friends and relatives had completely different notions as how to handle certain passages. I learned quickly that I could not accommodate everyone and to even attempt to do so would be the destruction of the whole effort.

Now that the manuscript is done and edited. I face the next problem. If the book sells moderately or well, should I write the next obvious part, my college years, learning to fly, the Army during Vietnam, my concluding college years after the Army and early married life?

I can remember a multitude of  great anecdotes while learning my trade in radio and TV. In my twenties I had a growing and completely negative attitude toward Catholicism and mysticism in general as a result of reading and discussing the ideas of Bertrand Russell, Ayn Rand, George Smith, Robert Ingersoll. These intellects and simple logic, learned in sophomore year in college, advanced all of the rational and atheistic ideas I had acquired in school earlier. My studies and continued analysis of mysticism changed my attitude toward religion. Instead of regarding it as merely a silly, baseless philosophy which I could reject and forget, it gradually dawned on me that religion had through history and does to this day have a major corrosive effect upon mankind. It makes its best adherents into fanatics who fly modern jets into large buildings.

I also met many new friends, some of whom were extremely influential to my philosophical manner of dealing with life in the latter part of the 20th Century. So once again there is no problem with finding things to write about that are interesting and very humorous. People have always seemed to say the most intimate things to me as if they know I will not spread what they told me to everyone. Well, now it's time to do some spreading! The market will tell me which way I ought to go.

Written by Ben Archer
Final edit 4-14-19
Bellingham, WA

Ben Archer grew up in a suburb of Chicago. He attended the University of Illinois. After three years in the Army he returned to college at the University of Hawaii. He married, had three beautiful kinds and never worked a day in his life because he was a radio talk show host in both Honolulu and Alaska. *From Here To Puberty* is his first book.

56973815R00124

Made in the USA
Columbia, SC
05 May 2019